The Dreadful River Cave

AND THERE IN THAT STRIP OF SANDY SHORE WE FOUND
THE IMPRINTS OF BARE FEET! (*page* 35)

The Dreadful River Cave

Chief Black Elk's Story

BY

JAMES WILLARD SCHULTZ

ILLUSTRATIONS BY HAROLD CUE

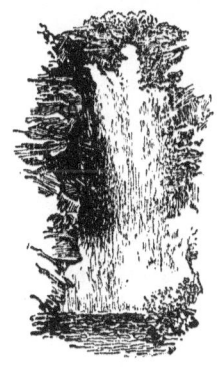

WILDSIDE PRESS

PREFACE

WHERE now rises the smoke from the hotels in Glacier National Park, once arose the smoke of our lodge fires; and now the motor-cars of the tourists whiz over the trails along which we rode upon our plodding hunting horses. There camping one time with Black Elk, he told me this tale of the Dreadful River Cave. I never attempted to enter the cave, but how many, many times I have paused at the foot of its falls, watching the trout in the deep, clear pool, occasionally glimpsing an otter or beaver, and sometimes larger game. That was more than forty years ago. In recent years some one named that outpouring of water from the face of the cliff, our Running Eagle Falls, "Trick Falls"! Our Rising Bull Mountain is now "Mount Rockwell"! Jealous Woman's Lake is now "McDermott's Lake"! Our ancient names for nearly all the mountains, lakes, and streams of that wonderful region have been taken from us. We have petitioned the Secretary of the Interior, all the powers-that-be in Washington, even the President, to restore them, but so far our efforts have been without result. My Blackfeet people say: "The whites have taken from us our game, our lands, utterly destroyed the trail that Sun marked out for us to follow, and now they take from us the

Preface

names of our mountains. It is that they wish to obliterate all knowledge of the fact that we once owned this great country!"

You who read this tale, who visit the mountains and streams that we once owned, will you not take a few minutes of your time to write your Senators and Congressmen to restore to them their ancient names?

JAMES WILLARD SCHULTZ

(APIKUNI)

University Club, Los Angeles
  August 1, 1920

CONTENTS

ILLUSTRATIONS

Drawn by HAROLD CUE

The Dreadful River Cave

. .

CHAPTER I

I HAVE marked the winters upon the edge of
this ancient bow of mine. It was my grandfather's bow; he made it in the days of his youth, and
in his old age gave it to me. I made this first little
crease in it to mark my eighteenth winter, the winter in which I for the first time met the enemy —
they were a war party of Crows — and fought them,
and took my first scalp. Count the creases; see,
there are five tens, and one; it is, then, just fifty
winters ago this very Moon of New Grass that we
experienced a day of terrible disasters.

We were encamped, five hundred and more lodges
of us, in the timbered bottom lands where Badger
River and Two Medicine River unite to make Bear
River.[1]

Heavy Runner was the chief of our clan, the
Small Robes. His head wife, Sings-at-the-Door, a
woman of fine character, of great and generous
heart, a woman loved and honored by us all, was

[1] The Marias River, Montana.

I

The Dreadful River Cave

very ill. This and that doctor woman had been called in to feed to her strong and bitter steepings of roots and leaves and barks, but she grew steadily worse. Then came the medicine men, one after another, and performed each one his own peculiar ceremony of prayers and songs and smoke offerings to the sun for her recovery, but still she grew worse. My father, Bear Eagle, was a powerful medicine man, owner of the beaver, or in other words the water, medicine pipe. He was the last one called in to the lodge of the sick one, and he had my mother and another medicine man, Old Sun, and his head wife, assist him. All night long, after painting the face and hands and feet of the sick one with the sacred color, they prayed and sang and smoked for her recovery, and soon after sunrise she died, yes, died while calling upon her man to hold her closer — to do his best to keep her shadow from setting out upon the long trail to the dreary Sand Hills.

She died, and Heavy Runner gently laid her body back upon the couch, and went outside and raised his hands to the sky and began to curse the sun. I cannot, I dare not, tell you what he said. Never before had any of our people done such a terrible thing as that. Some who heard him stopped their ears to the sound of his words; others ran away that they might hear no more. Long he stood there, calling the sun all the bad names that he could think of, defying him to do further harm,

Dreadful Cave and a Water God

and then he turned and called out to his young wives: "Prepare the body of my dear one for burial! I go to drive in some of my horses to kill at her burial-place!"

"You, my father, rest! I will go for the horses. Oh, my father, rest and beg the sun to forgive you your bad words!" one of his sons said to him. But Heavy Runner appeared not to see him nor to have heard him. He started to walk out through the camp, made a few steps, and fell, and was dead before any one could reach his side. The women, wailing, mourning now for two loved ones, bore the body into the lodge and began to prepare it, too, for burial. Gloom settled down upon the whole camp; we could think of nothing but the swift and terrible punishment the sun had inflicted upon the chief. Even the little children sat quiet, frightened of they knew not what. The camp dogs whined, and sneaked uneasily, fearfully, from group to group, their tails tight down between their legs.

And now straight in through the camp to the lodges of our Small Robes clan came a lone warrior, Yellow Plume, thus wailing: "Alas! Alas! Alas! I am the sole survivor of our party! Near the Falls of Big River, at night, a large party of the enemy surprised us! We fought bravely, but they were a multitude, we but twelve men. I alone survive!"

And with that down he sat in front of the lodge of our dead chief, his hair all undone and

The Dreadful River Cave

tangled, his face and hands black painted, and wailed, and the parents and wives and children and sweethearts and friends of his dead comrades wailed with him, calling out over and over again the names of their lost ones. And presently the warrior stood up and thrust the hair back from his face and called out to my father: "Bear Eagle, medicine man, what think you now of your water medicine? You gave us the sacred sweat bath upon the day of our departure! We smoked your water pipe to the sun, and you assured us that we would be successful. Ha! Successful! Bear Eagle, I tell you now that your pipe has lost its power!"

What answer could my father make to that? The sick woman had died while he was praying for her! Eleven fine, brave warriors for whom he had made medicine, and for whom he had prayed every evening since their departure, were also dead! Standing there listening to the lone survivor of the party he seemed suddenly to grow old. His face turned gray; his erect, strong body suddenly drooped. Without a word he turned and went slowly, feebly, into our lodge. The lone warrior sat down again and resumed his wailing.

In the afternoon the well-wrapped bodies of the chief and the woman were taken up-river and lashed upon a platform of poles built in a big cottonwood tree, and four horses were killed under it. All day long the people mourned for their dead. At sunset there came into camp seven of a party of

Dreadful Cave and a Water God

twenty-three warriors that had gone, a moon back, east to war against the Assiniboines. They, too, had been ambushed by superior numbers of the enemy, and only the seven had survived the sudden attack. And so, with the gathering night, there was increased mourning in our great camp. People began to say to one another that it seemed as though the gods had forsaken us.

Old Sun had been the medicine man for the war party that went against the Assiniboines. The seven survivors blamed him for what had happened; they said that his thunder medicine pipe had lost its power. Like my father, he was so distressed that he could neither eat nor sleep. In the evening of the day after the burial of our chief and his woman, Old Sun came into our lodge. My father motioned him to a seat, filled and lighted a pipe and passed it to him. They smoked slowly, by turns, saying never a word. None of us spoke. The silence became almost unbearable. I felt that I could not stand it.

I was preparing to go out and wander about in camp when Old Sun said to my father: "My friend, what terrible misfortune has come upon you and me! Never were there more powerful medicines than ours, and suddenly they have failed us. Instead of life and success, death comes to those who seek our aid. Now, what is it, think you, that is the cause of this?"

"I have thought about and thought about it,

5

The Dreadful River Cave

and can see no light. I am almost crazy!" my father answered.

"Well, I will tell you what I think," said Old Sun. "I believe that the tobacco we are using in our medicine pipes is offensive to the gods; that they cannot bear the odor of the smoke of it. Have n't you noticed how stifling the odor is, and how bitter the taste of the smoke?"

"It is bitter; bad-odored. I believe that you are right; if it is offensive to us, it must be still more offensive to the gods. Why, my friend, it may even be that the trader from whom we got it put some of his bad white medicine in it on purpose to bring us bad luck!"

"No, he would not do that. I am sure he is our friend. His Mandan wife speaks well of him," said Old Sun.

They were speaking of Ki-pah,[1] a chief of the Long Knives Company, who had the summer before come up with men and boats and trade goods, from the Great House at the mouth of the Yellowstone, and built a trading-post at the mouth of Bear River.

"Well it may be that bad medicine was put into the tobacco before he got it," said my father. "Anyhow, we must use no more of it. My friend, there is but one thing for us to do: hereafter we

---

[1] Captain James Kipp, who built the American Fur Company's post, Fort MacKenzie, at the junction of the Marias and Missouri Rivers, in 1833.

Dreadful Cave and a Water God

must use nothing but our own, our ancient nah-wak'-o-sis in our medicine ceremonies. Thus will we get back the favor of the gods."

"But there is so little of it; none has been planted by any of our people for many summers," Old Sun objected.

"I still have some; you shall have half of it. And I know that the widow of our old friend, Little Wolf, has a large sack of the seed. My friend, listen: We must get that seed from her and plant it and raise a big crop of the leaves," said my father.

"Yes, and then go away, and return to find that the grasshoppers and the deer have eaten about all of it!"

"No!" my father cried, suddenly straightening up and loudly clapping his hands together. "No! This is so important to us that we must take no chances. We will select a favorable place and plant the seed, and stay right there and help it grow, protecting the young leaves from all who would devour them."

"And ourselves probably be wiped out by some passing war party of the enemy!"

"We must take that risk!" said my father. "However, if we are cautious the risk will not be very great. I propose that we move up into the timber that surrounds the lower Two Medicine Lake, and send our horses right back to be herded by some of our relatives. There are many sunny,

The Dreadful River Cave

warm, open places in that timber where our planting will grow well."

"Good! Let us do that, provided we can get the seed," said Old Sun.

My father sent my mother to question the old widow, Red Wing Woman, and she soon returned with her, the latter carrying the skin of an antelope fawn stuffed full, legs and all, so that it had almost the appearance of life.

"Oh, great medicine men, how happy your message makes me feel!" the old woman cried. "Long, long have I been saving this sacred seed, hoping that some one would plant it. And now you will do that! Oh, take it! Plant it all! Oh, just see what good seed it is!" And with that she thrust her hand into the mouth of the stuffed skin and brought it out filled with large, thin, gray-white seeds, exposed them to our view, then replaced them and laid the skin before my father.

"Oh, the gods love nah-wak'-o-sis!" she cried. "Old Man himself made the seed and planted it, and Sun warmed it and made it sprout and burst up through the ground and grow into large and perfect leaf and seed for the use of our first fathers. And it has been used by our tribe ever since that long-ago time, and all has been well with us until you medicine men laid it aside, and filled your lodges with the strong, bad odor of the white traders' weed!"

"Good woman, you speak the truth," Old Sun told her.

8

Dreadful Cave and a Water God

"Gladly we take this seed," my father said, "and shall plant it and tend the growing plants with our best care, and in the Moon of Falling Leaves give back to you as much as you have given us."

My mother prepared a little feast for the old woman. My father and Old Sun went over to the lodge of Lone Walker, our head chief, to talk with him about their plan, and I went with them. Lone Walker at once called a council of all the clan chiefs. They all agreed that the very life of the tribe depended upon the renewed use of nah-wak'-o-sis by the medicine men, but some maintained that the seed should be planted with the usual ceremonies, and then left to grow as it would. They feared that if the two families of us remained with the planting we should be discovered by the enemy and killed; the lives of medicine men were too valuable to the tribe to be risked in any such manner. After much talk my father and Old Sun got their way in the matter. It was agreed that the tribe should move to Point-of-Rocks River,[1] and then south to the Belt Mountains for the summer, and in the Moon of Falling Leaves come north to Two Medicine where we should rejoin them.

On the very next day the two families of us started for Two Medicine Lake, two of my cousins and a nephew of Old Sun going with us to bring out our horses and care for them during the summer. We had no more than left the great camp than

[1] Sun River.

9

The Dreadful River Cave

we were overtaken by Red Wing Woman and her granddaughter, Dove Woman, a very beautiful girl of nearly my age. The old woman rode up close beside my father and Old Sun, crying out to them: "Oh, great medicine men! Here we are, you see, our lodge and all well packed upon our horses. I want to help you plant and raise the nah-wak'-o-sis. Do not be stone-hearted! Allow us to go with you!"

My father looked questioningly at Old Sun, who nodded his head, and then he answered the old woman: "We are glad that you are coming with us. You are furnishing the sacred seed, and we shall be very glad to have you help us in our summer's work."

"Ha! I thought you would say something like that," the old woman cried, and was so happy that she began singing, and kept on singing one song and another all the morning.

Well, in the afternoon of the following day we rode down into the deep valley of the Two Medicine, crossed the river just below the lower lake, then a bit of prairie, and sought a good gardening-and camping-place in the heavy timber sloping up to the bare rocks of the mountain heights. Search as we would we could not find a favorable place. We turned about, recrossed the river, and wended our way up a heavy game trail running close beside the lake. This slope of the valley was sunny and warm, supporting fine growths of quaking aspen

Dreadful Cave and a Water God

and cottonwood as well as open groves of pine and fir. Near the head of the lake we left the trail, followed up a small stream to a big spring, and there made camp. Below the spring there was an almost level space of ground much larger than we needed for our planting. We had but to cut a few quaking aspens that grew upon it, and the moist, dark, leaf-strewn and almost grassless earth would be exposed to the sun all day long. We put up our three lodges in the shelter of some very large cottonwoods that stood just above the spring. Our location was just about halfway from the lake to the top of the long ridge sloping from the plain up to the foot of an outer, bare-peaked mountain of the great range, the Backbone-of-the-World.

Early on the following morning our relatives rounded up our horses and started homeward with them. Much against my father's and Old Sun's wishes I kept out two, which I picketed some distance back from camp. I insisted that I must have them for packing in the meat that I should kill; that I could not possibly pack in upon my own back sufficient food for three lodges of people. Old Sun, his head wife, North Woman, his younger wives, Fine Robe Woman and Arrow Woman, and five children, were nine. Red Wing Woman and her granddaughter were two. My father and his head wife — my mother, Sings Alone Woman, and my almost-mothers, Running Woman and Little Fox Woman, and their five children, and I were ten. I

The Dreadful River Cave

had to kill meat for twenty-one people. Do you wonder that I kept back two horses, one to ride and one to pack?

"Some day a war party will come upon your horses' tracks and follow them right to our camp!" my father said.

"I shall keep off the trails. When I have to cross one I shall get down and smooth it over," I answered.

"Horses can be seen a long way off," said Old Sun.

"Not mine: I shall keep them picketed in the timber, and never ride them out upon open country," I replied.

That very day the women cut down the quaking aspens standing upon the space of ground that my father and Old Sun marked for the planting, and having dragged them out of the way they began piling dry brush in the cleared space, which was about seventy-five paces long and fifty paces wide. They soon collected all that lay near by, and were then glad enough to use my horses to drag in heavy dry limbs and fallen tree-tops from some distance around. They continued this work all of the next day, and by evening had covered the whole space with a closely packed, breast-high layer of brush. It was past midnight, a time when a blaze would be least likely to be seen by the enemy, that we took some burning sticks from our lodge fires and, running swiftly, dropped them here and there along

Dreadful Cave and a Water God

the edge of the brush-pile. What a fire it made; so hot that we retreated to our lodges for protection. It roared as loudly as a big waterfall, and made the whole ridge-side as light as day; and it burned a long time; day was breaking when the last of the larger limbs were consumed and the embers ceased to smoke. My father and Old Sun then went to the edge of the burning and dug into it with sharp sticks, finding that even at an arm's length down the earth was unbearably hot. There was no doubt but every life root of every weed and tuft of grass in the burned space had been killed. In the ashes-enriched, clean earth our nah-wak'-o-sis plants would have no enemies, and would surely attain full growth and go to seed before the coming of the frost.

We waited a day and night for the burned earth to cool, and then the women began prying it up and turning it over with sharp sticks and buffalo shoulder blades, making it all of a fineness suitable for the planting of our seeds. We were now nearly out of meat, so I saddled one of my horses and started out to get some. I had a fine new gun, a flintlock smoothbore which I had bought of the trader at the mouth of Bear River, and I took it with me as well as the bow and arrows my grandfather had given me. In those days we used the bow in preference to the gun for two reasons: because it was noiseless, and because powder and ball were very costly and only to be obtained by long journeys

The Dreadful River Cave

across the plains to the Red Coat traders of the North or the Long Knives on Big River.

I was no more than out of sight of camp than the horse I had left there began to nicker loudly for its mate, and it, too, as loudly answer, and prance and kick, and endeavor to turn and carry me back to camp. I forced it to go on, but it would not cease nickering, and pretending to be afraid of everything it saw ahead, rocks, stumps, a fallen branch, making so much noise that it would frighten off any game animals long before I could see them. It was useless to go on. I turned back, intending to re-picket the horse and hunt on foot, when I saw Dove Woman riding swiftly toward me through the timber on the other horse. She came to my side and the animals gave several last, low, satisfied nickers and rubbed noses.

"Oh, Black Elk, almost-brother," she said, "they cried out that the horses were making too much enemy-attracting noise, and ordered me to go with you and help you butcher and bring in your kills. I am glad! I hate ground-digging work!"

"Ha! I never thought that you were lazy! Be ashamed of yourself!" I told her.

"I am not lazy!" she cried. "It is just that I was born wrong. I hate women's work. I should have been a boy. I love to ride; to follow the hunters. I want to have weapons and kill meat for my grandmother and myself!"

The girl's earnestness pleased me; her eyes were

Dreadful Cave and a Water God

afire with resentment. "Almost-sister," I said, "during these summer moons you shall be a hunter; you shall hunt with me. I really need your help. Come. We will go down into the valley and try to kill a moose or an elk!"

We rode slanting down the ridge to strike the valley just above the head of the lower lake. When near the foot of the slope we dismounted, picketed the horses, went on afoot, and crossed the deep, well-worn trail that ran from the plains up through the great range and down its western slope. It was a great game trail, and was used at times by West Side tribes, Snakes, Kalispels, Pend d'Oreilles, Nez Percés, and Kootenais coming out to hunt buffaloes upon our plains. At this time we were at war with all but the Kootenais. With them we had been ever friendly, and were always glad to have them come out from their mountain country to camp and hunt with us.

We carefully examined the trail, found no signs of passing enemies upon it, and went on down to a beaver pond just above the head of the lake. This was the largest beaver pond in all our country. The high, broad dam extended clear across the valley and was so old that many full-grown cottonwood trees stood upon it. Four or five sluiceways in good repair along the dam provided passage for the flow of the river water and assured its safety in times of flood. There were many beaver houses in the pond and we saw some of the animals swim-

The Dreadful River Cave

ming among them. I had three traps, and made up my mind to use them here.

Both above and below the pond were dense growths of willows in among the cottonwoods, fine feeding- and resting-places for moose and elk. We skirted the edge of the pond and entered the willow swamp above it, finding it criss-crossed with trails of game, not only moose and elk, deer and buffaloes, but bears as well. Following one of these trails leading into the heart of the swamp, I soon came upon the tracks of a bear that were almost twice the length of my footprints. I pointed to them and asked Dove Woman if she felt like going on. She shivered a little and answered: "Of course I have fear, but you lead on. I shall follow you!"

I was not very much afraid. It is true that grizzly bears will sometimes attack a hunter without provocation, but generally they will run away the instant they get sight or odor of man. I handed my gun to the girl, drew my bow and several arrows from the case at my back and led on. If I was to sight game it would be so close that an arrow would be as effective as a bullet. "Keep close to me and be ready to hand me the gun if I need it," I told the girl.

The trail soon forked. The huge bear tracks continued along the left fork. I am not ashamed to say that I breathed more easily as I turned into the right fork. We had not gone far along the fork when I saw, close ahead, some willows quiver. I

Dreadful Cave and a Water God

stopped short, bow ready, and presently a bull moose came in sight, only his head and the top of his back visible above a clump of red willows standing between two dense high growths of black willows. The moose stopped there and began nipping off the tender top shoots of the red willows. I thought that my one chance was to shoot at him where he stood, for he was already looking straight at me. I aimed my arrow to slip through the brush and strike into his side just back of the shoulder and low down, and let it go with all my strength. I saw the moose flinch and knew that I had hit him. Before I could fit another arrow to the bow he had disappeared, running straight from me. We ran ahead through the brush, struck his trail and followed it. There was very little blood along it, only a few drops here and there, and from the start I felt that I had only slightly wounded the animal and would be unable to get another shot at him. He led us toward the river, and then up along a game trail close beside it, and kept going at a steady trot, as we could see by his tracks. After a time we could find no more droppings of blood and I gave up the chase, although Dove Woman, still very much excited, urged that we keep on after him. I pointed to the steep side hill up which he had turned from the trail: "It is just wasting the day to follow him farther. His climbing that steep place is proof enough that my arrow gave him no more than a flesh wound," I told her.

The Dreadful River Cave

We were now quite near the waterfall between the two lakes; could plainly hear its roar. Time and time again I had been within hearing of it, but had never seen it. I had heard much talk about it. Some of our old men advised us never to go near it because it was the home of some of the Under-Water People. I determined now at least to have a look at it, and asked Dove Woman if she felt like following me. She told me to lead on; that wherever I went she would be right close behind me.

We went on up the now narrow cañon, turned a point of rock and faced a high cliff abruptly ending the cañon. A little water was pouring from the top of it into a deep pool at its base. The greater part of the river was gushing from a wide, dark cavern in the cliff, about a third of the way up its face, and cascading down into the pool. It was in this cavern that the old men claimed the Under-Water People lived. From where we stood, the water falling from the top of the cliff hid the left part of the cavern from us. But as I looked I thought that I saw, dimly through the falling mist, something moving up along the edge of the main fall, something that had the shape of a man.

CHAPTER II

PERHAPS my eyes deceived me. That any living thing other than an otter would attempt to enter that dark cavern of roaring, rushing water was unbelievable. I glanced over my shoulder at Dove Woman, standing just back of me and to my left. She was staring wide-eyed, open-mouthed, at the fall. I looked again at it; tried to pierce the darkness behind the down-fluttering, swaying mist from the upper fall and could see nothing but black rock and white, foaming water. I turned again to Dove Woman. She raised her hand and pointed to the dark cavern; she spoke, but I could not hear her.

"What did you say?" I shouted, moving closer to her.

"Did n't you see it?" she cried. "There back of the spray; a person moving up along the edge of the out-rushing water; disappearing into the black night of the cave!" She turned and ran back down the rocky shore of the river. I looked again at the fall, then followed and overtook her behind the point of rock. I signed to her to follow me, and turned straight up the steep cañon side, and then moved off to the left and crouched behind a patch of junipers through which I could plainly see the falls. She seated herself at my side.

19

The Dreadful River Cave

"You are sure that you saw some one going into that black hole in the cliff?" I asked.

"Just as sure as I am that I sit here beside you," she answered.

"Well, I thought that I saw something in there, dark, man-shaped, but I could not believe that I saw it. Even now I doubt that any one can go into that place," I told her.

"The Under-Water People can go wherever there is water!" she said.

"But they do not walk, they swim. In all the tales about them that have been handed down to us there is no mention of them walking or of even coming out from the water," I objected.

"That is no proof that they don't come out of the water and walk about. Say what you will, I know what I know. I saw one of the Under-Water People walking into that hole in the cliff."

"Well, let us not argue about it. We will sit here for a time and watch for the person to come out," I told her.

"I have not told you all that I saw: the Under-Water person had on a leather robe, red-painted," she said.

I did not answer that. I knew not what to think; my mind was all confused. A big splash of water in the lower end of the pool at the foot of the cliff made us both start. "See! There! The Under-Water person!" the girl hissed in my ear.

I laid down my bow and arrows and took my gun

How Dreadful Cave was Made

from her. Our warriors had never killed nor attempted to kill one of these Under-Water People. It was possible that their medicine made their bodies proof against our weapons. But I was determined to do my best to kill this one when he reappeared. I cocked the gun, made sure that the pan was full of powder, and watched the pool. Out in the center the water suddenly heaved and swirled: "See! He is swimming about in there. He will soon appear!" the girl said to me.

And she had no more than spoken when a large otter shot up from the depths with a trout held fast in its jaws, and swam to a rock sloping out of the water at the foot of the pool, and climbed out upon it. There it released the wiggling trout only to seize it by the head and kill it, then looked toward some bushes growing thick upon the shore. We could not hear the call it made, but at once three young otters came out from under the brush and swam toward the rock, and when they were quite near it the old one slipped into the water and led them off downstream and around a bend out of our sight.

"Well, almost-sister, there went our Under-Water person!" I said, handing her back the gun, and taking up my bow and arrows.

"No!" she cried. "Of course it was the otter that made that big splash in the pool, but just as surely as I see you, I saw a red-robed person go into the darkness of that hole in the cliff!"

I had to believe that she was not mistaken. Had

The Dreadful River Cave

not I, myself, thought that I had seen a person behind the spray from the upper fall?

"I do believe you," I told her. "But we must go:
we have many hungry mouths to feed. As soon as
we have a good supply of meat in camp we will
come here again and watch for the Under-Water
person."

We went up out of the cañon, crossed the big
trail, and began hunting along the slope of the ridge
toward our horses. Signs of game were almost as
plentiful as they were down in the willow swamp,
and it was not long before I sighted meat, two buffalo bulls feeding in a little grassy park in the timber. By sneaking from one patch of brush to another, and sometimes crawling upon hands and
knees, we made our way to the foot of the park
without alarming them. They were feeding straight
down through the center of the opening, evidently
upon their way to water, so we each got behind a
big tree and waited for them to come on. I soon saw
that they would pass so close in front of me that I
could almost reach out and touch them, and felt
sure that I could kill them both. I waited until the
lead bull was two or three steps past me and then
sent an arrow into his side, well down and just back
of the ribs. He was done for, I knew. I had not to
pay any more attention to him. I fitted another
arrow to my bow, and just as I let it go at the
other bull, Dove Woman fired my gun at him and
he fell dead, shot through the heart.

How Dreadful Cave was Made

"I killed him! I killed him!" she cried, running out from behind her tree and dancing around the big animal.

"But you should n't have done it. I am much displeased with you! That boom of the gun may have reached the ears of some enemy!" I told her.

"Almost-brother, don't be angry," she pleaded. "I just could n't help it! All my life long I have wanted to kill a buffalo. And there I was with the gun in my hands, and the bull passing so close — why, it seems as if the gun came up against my shoulder without the least help from me!"

"And no doubt cocked itself and pulled its own trigger!" I said.

And then we both laughed. I could not be angry with her, spoil her happiness. She was so excited over her success that she was actually trembling. I took the gun from her, reloaded it, and then we butchered first her kill, and then mine, lying close by. The animals were so fat that we cut up all the meat of them and tied the pieces suitably for packing. We then got our horses, loaded them with all the weight that they could carry and led them up the ridge to camp.

All the women were at work in the burned-over place, preparing the earth for the sacred planting. My father and Old Sun were having a medicine smoke. We did not speak to any of them, unloading our horses as quickly as we could and going straight back for more meat. In all we made four trips to

The Dreadful River Cave

camp, each time with all the meat the horses could carry. The sun was setting when we brought in the last of it, and we were tired enough.

After the evening meal, when all the members of our little camp had gathered in my father's lodge to pass the time, Dove Woman and I told our adventures of the day. All listened with close attention and many exclamations of surprise, and my father and Old Sun questioned us closely and made us describe over and over again all that we had seen at the falls.

Said Old Sun, when we had finished: "It is well known that that hole in the cliff from which the river gushes is inhabited by Under-Water People. From our first fathers the tale has come down to us that, in the beginning, no cliff was there. When Old Man made the world, he made a straight, smooth, deep valley there, beginning it at the summit of the mountains and extending it out across the plains. He had, of course, first made the mountains. But he was sometimes careless in his work. Just here, to the right of the valley, he had made a high, slender mountain and failed to set it straight up; it leaned to the south; and after he had made the valley it toppled over, forming this rock wall across it. Above, among the big loose rocks that filled the valley, the river sank out of sight, only to reappear gushing from the dark hole in the wall. When Old Man returned to this place and saw what had happened he blamed himself.

How Dreadful Cave was Made

Said he: 'I should have been more careful. If I had set that mountain straight up like the others it would not have fallen. In my haste I only made more work for myself. I have now to clear the valley of this great mass of rock that fills it.'

"But just then he saw that the fallen mountain had not stopped the flow of the river; saw its waters gushing from the strange, dark hole in the wall rock. 'Ha! It is best that I leave this falling just as it is,' he said. 'That hole in there, and the deep pool below, will be a good home for some of my Under-Water People.' And with that he turned about and went off to other of his world-making work.

"Old Man, remember, had already made Under-Water People, and given them the water for their country, and the life that is in it for their food. He did not make our ancestors until he had completed his world-making. Nor did he intend, I feel sure, that the Under-Water People and we should be enemies. But enemies we are — oh, how many of us they have seized and drawn down to death in the deep water of the rivers — and so, my children, you must keep away from that river cave."

"I cannot believe that it was an Under-Water person we saw," I said. "I had but a dim, shadowy glimpse of something behind the falling spray, but almost-sister, who was off to my left, says that she saw him plainly, and that he was wearing a red-painted robe. To me it does n't seem possible that

25

The Dreadful River Cave

an Under-Water person could wear a robe. He could not swim with it, and, once wet, it would be no protection from the cold."

"My son," my father answered me, "with those dwellers in the deep waters all things are possible. You forget that tale of our ancestor who visited them in the long ago. Down at the bottom of the river they were living in warm, comfortable lodges and wearing beautiful clothing of furs and leather. Even more strange than that, they gave him a feast of red, sun-ripened strawberries. Why, then, should not the one you saw to-day have had on a dry, red-painted robe, even though he had come up out of the water with it?"

I could make no answer to that. The old men talked on and on. The women chatted together. It was quite late when our visitors went to their lodges and we lay down upon our couches. It was long before I slept. The more I thought about it, the more convinced I was that he whom we had seen was no Under-Water person. I believed that he was a dweller upon the earth. Perhaps a member of one of our tribes, more likely a member of one of the West-Side tribes with which we were at war. I decided that I would go again and again to the falls and watch for the frequenter of the dark river cave.

The next morning the women had to cut the buffalo meat into thin sheets for drying before resuming their work in the planting-place. As soon as our early meal was over I watered my horses, picketed

26

How Dreadful Cave was Made

them upon fresh grass, then slung my bow-case over my shoulder and took up my gun and started out of camp. As I passed my father and Old Sun, sitting out in the sun and smoking and talking, they looked up and Old Sun asked where I was going.

"Oh, just out on discovery, to see if there are signs of any enemies about," I answered.

"Go not near that Under-Water person's cave!" my father commanded, and to that I made no reply. As I passed the meat-cutters Dove Woman looked up and signed that she would go with me.

"No! I go alone!" I signed back to her, and went on along the slope of the ridge. But as soon as I was out of sight of camp I turned down it toward the falls, following the trail that Dove Woman and I had made the day before when bringing in the loads of meat. As I neared the place where we had made the kills I moved more and more slowly, thinking that I might see some wolves feeding upon the remains of the carcasses. Not that I wanted to kill them, but because I loved always to watch them, wisest, I thought, of all the four-footed hunters that roamed our plains and mountains. So, when quite near the little park in the timber, I got down upon my hands and knees and crawled on through the grass and brush, and presently heard loud crunching of bones; hollow champing of jaws and sucking smacking of lips.

"Wolves are there; feeding upon the bones and

The Dreadful River Cave

shreds of meat that we left," I said to myself, and was glad that I was approaching the park so quietly and would see the animals.

I was now only a few steps from the edge of the park, but could not see it through the thick brush. I crawled on still more slowly, making no noise, and at last looked out from some red willows, and went suddenly all cold at what I saw there: an immense bear feeding upon the backbone and head of one of the bulls that we had killed. And near him lay the backbone and head of the other bull; he had dragged them both from the timber below out to the center of the open park for his feasting-place. He was the largest bear that I had ever seen: maker, no doubt, of the tracks that we had followed the day before. I did not know what to do. I wanted to kill him; wanted his immense claws for a necklace. But what a terrible risk I should be taking if my one shot failed to drop him where he stood. I thought of this hunter and that hunter killed by bears. I concluded to sneak away and leave him to his feasting, and did crawl back a little way; then called myself a coward and returned to the red willows.

Noiselessly I cocked my gun and examined the pan; it was full of powder. I slowly arose upon my knees and was raising the gun to take aim, when the bear suddenly raised his head and stared off toward the foot of the little park, his hair all bristling forward as he gave two or three snorts of anger. I looked off in that direction and saw a large

How Dreadful Cave was Made ¹

bear come out from the brush into the park, walking steadily toward the one in front of me. Turning again to him, still angrily snorting and growling and staring at the newcomer, I saw him suddenly become quiet; his hair smoothed back into place and he resumed his feasting. I looked back down the park and saw that three cubs had come out of the brush. Then all was clear to me: the newcomer was the big one's wife; he had not recognized her until the young ones appeared, and then he had calmed down. She was welcome to his feast.

"This is no place for me. I should have risked a shot at the old chief bear, but two of them — " I said to myself, and backed out into the timber and was glad enough when I at last got upon my feet and was sure that I should not be pursued.

But presently as I went on toward the falls I began to feel some doubt of myself; to wonder if I had not been somewhat cowardly. I did not want to be a coward; that I hated above all things. I took some comfort by saying that I should find a way to count *coup* upon the big bear, and began to plan how to do it.

Now that I was not in quest of meat I saw plenty of it as I went on through the timber, several small bands of elk and deer along the ridge, and a cow and a yearling moose in the edge of the swamp at the upper end of the big beaver pond. Some beavers swimming about among their lodges reminded me that I had forgotten to bring my traps.

The Dreadful River Cave

Passing the swamp and following up the river, I entered the narrow cañon, and at the point of rock turned up the steep side, took shelter behind the patch of junipers and looked through them down at the falls; no one, man of the earth nor man of the waters, was in sight and I felt somewhat disappointed. I stretched myself out as comfortably as I could upon the hard rock, determined to remain right there and watch the falls until night.

The sun moved on and on up into the blue and made the day warm. I became sleepy; could not help dozing now and then, but always for a very short time. I would know when I was about to sleep soundly, and then would force myself to open my eyes and look down again at the falls. After the sun had passed the middle of the blue I was having a short half-sleep when I felt myself suddenly seized by the ankle. I cried out sharply, whirled about gun in hand, and instead of the enemy that I expected to see found myself staring into Dove Woman's laughing face!

"Oh, how I frightened you!" she said.

"You did!" I angrily answered. "And you should n't have done it! I might have shot you before I saw who you were! Don't you ever do that to me again!"

"No! Never! Never, almost-brother. Oh, don't be angry at me," she pleaded. And then, when I saw tears in her eyes, I took shame for scolding her, and still more shame for having slept when I

How Dreadful Cave was Made

should have had my eyes constantly upon the river cave.

"Don't cry! My anger is gone. I feel sorry for you. A fine scolding you will get when we return home this evening. You sneaked out of camp!" I told her.

"You will take my part. You will speak soft words to them," she said, and I knew that I should.

"What way did you come — by our kills of yesterday?" I asked.

"No. I did not want to go near the beaver-pond swamps. I went straight out from camp along the ridge, and then turned straight down hill to the mouth of the cañon," she explained.

"The gods directed your steps!" I said. "I followed the trail to our kills: heard crunching of bones in the little park, got down upon hands and knees and sneaked to the edge of it, and saw, not wolves, as I expected, but the big bear of the swamp and his wife and three children."

"And then — what did you?" she whispered, staring at me with wide-open, frightened eyes.

"Turned coward! The old chief bear was feasting upon the backbone and head of one of the bulls that he had bagged up into the park. His wife and children were approaching him. I sneaked away from there as quietly as I could. Almost-sister, had you gone hurrying along there you would doubtless have been torn to pieces. Old mother bears, you know, are fierce protectors of their young!"

The Dreadful River Cave

Dove Woman shivered. "Almost I went that way! The gods must have turned me from the trail," she said, so low that I could no more than hear her. And then: "Why say that you were a coward? Well you know that not a single hunter of our three tribes would have attacked that big bear and his wife!"

"We will say nothing about them when we return home. I am planning to get that big bear. I must have his claws for a necklace before we leave this valley," I told her.

"But this I shall do this very evening," I went on. "I shall tell my father that I intend to watch this place until I know who it is lives in the cave behind the falls, and that you are to watch with me!"

"Yes, do that!" she said. "I hate sneaking out from camp; the thought of the scolding I shall get upon my return spoils all my pleasure of the day."

We spoke no more for a time. I turned back, stretched out upon the rock to watch the falls, and the girl sat beside me. I had unslung my bow-case when I lay down, and she drew the bow and a couple of arrows from it and held them in her lap. She had great love for weapons.

The sun moved on down into the west. We remained motionless, silent. A warm wind came down the valley, a wind heavy with the pleasant odor of pine and balsam and the flowers of early summer. The waterfall sang to us with everchanging voice, sometimes low and sweet, and more

How Dreadful Cave was Made

often with a deep and powerful roar that somehow was oppressive. Swimming close inshore where was least current, a sharp-billed fish duck came up the stream followed by her brood of newborn young. They entered the big, deep, swirling pool at the foot of the falls and floated around and around upon it, the mother sometimes diving for a trout, but more often snapping one up from its hiding-place among the rocks in the shallow water close to shore. Very small were those she caught, so small that we could not see them as her young crowded and fluttered around and eagerly seized them from her bill.

One of the young, more adventurous than the others, suddenly left its mother's side and went swimming and flapping toward the center of the pool in pursuit of a trout or perhaps a water-bug. It lost sight of its prey and stopped, then beat the water with its wings and stretched out its neck and cried for help as something invisible to us began to drag it down. We could not hear its cries; the roar of the waterfall prevented their reaching our ears. But the mother heard and went swiftly to its aid; but before she could swim and flap halfway to it only a few bursting bubbles marked the place where it had been.

"The Under-Water person! It was he who seized the duck! We shall see him!" Dove Woman whispered to me, bending low at my side.

I thought as she did, but said nothing; kept my

The Dreadful River Cave

eyes upon the pool. The mother duck was wildly turning around and around looking for her missing one, her frightened young trying to keep close to her side. Then the water broke at the edge of the far side of the pool and a big otter drew out from it with the dead duckling in his mouth. He dropped it upon a flat rock and turned about and dived back into the pool, and off downstream went the mother duck with her young trailing after her. The otter soon stuck his head up out of the water, saw that they were gone, and turning back to shore took up his kill and swam off down-river with it.

"Oh, how low-hearted I am! I was sure that the duck-seizer was an Under-Water person, and that we were to see him!" said Dove Woman.

"Take courage!" I told her. It was all that I could say. I, too, was terribly disappointed.

Several times during the afternoon otters of different size came up into the pool, soon caught large trout, and went downstream with them. In under the big rocks that lay piled along the shores of the pool were good, dry places for them to make their homes and rear their young. I asked myself why they did not live there? The answer was plain: they were afraid to live so close to the dweller in the dark river cave!

Our long watch was now drawing to a close. The sun was about to trail down behind the mountains, and Dove Woman pointed to it and urged that we go. I knew her thought, and I myself did not care

How Dreadful Cave was Made

to risk meeting the big bear and his wife in the timber in the darkness of the night.

"Yes, we will go home," I told her, "but first we will go down to the pool and examine its shore."

She made no answer to that, but I saw her shiver as she arose to follow me. I led the way back down behind the point of rock to the shore of the river, and then up along it toward the falls. In places there was no shore, the bare rock of the cañon sloping steeply down into the water. We made our way along this with some difficulty, and at last stepped down upon a small, sandy, bush-grown point at the foot of the big pool. And there in that strip of sandy shore we found the imprints of bare feet! Dove Woman shrank back when she saw them and grasped my arm, and we stood a long time staring at them and at the river tumbling in white foam down the rocky slant from the hole in the cliff, half-hidden from us by the spray of water falling from the height above and swaying with the wind.

CHAPTER III

IF I had doubted that we actually had seen an Under-Water person going up into the dark cave my doubts were now gone. There were his tracks in the sand, fresh, plain imprints of feet no larger than mine and in no way different from them. I was somehow surprised that they were not different.

"Almost-brother, I am afraid! Let us go!" said Dove Woman close in my ear.

I turned at once and led the way back. I myself did not care to be standing so close to that black hole. Perhaps the Under-Water person was staring out at us from the darkness. There was no knowing what he, all powerful evil god of the water, might do to us if he saw us there. As we were rounding the point of rock I stopped Dove Woman and turned for a last look at the falls; no one was in sight there. I hoped that we had not been seen.

On our way home we circled away out around the place of our buffalo kills to avoid the bear family, and arrived in camp while there was still a little light in the western sky.

Old Red Wing Woman was standing outside her lodge and as soon as she saw us came running to Dove Woman, seized her by the arms fiercely and shook her. "Bad girl! Lazy girl!" she cried. "You

36

We Watch Dreadful Cave

will run away from your work! Just wait until I get hold of a stick and I shall give you the beating that you deserve!"

"No, no! Don't do that, almost-grandmother," I said, getting between her and the girl. "You well know that she is not bad, nor lazy. Come with us to my father's lodge. When you hear about the great discovery we have made you will be glad that she left her work and followed me."

"Oh! A great discovery! Useless, lazy wandering about, I am sure!" she cried, and followed us, muttering to herself.

When we went inside we found Old Sun and his family gathered there. My father and he paid no attention to us; my mother set plenty of food before us and went on talking with the other women. We ate heartily, leisurely, and when we could eat no more I sat back comfortably upon my couch and said: "Well, father, well, Old Sun, listen! We went again to the pool at the foot of the river cave cliff, and found there in a strip of sandy shore, fresh tracks of the Under-Water person."

"Ha!" the men exclaimed. The women gasped. All stared at me.

"I plainly told you not to go there again!" my father all but shouted to me.

"But I did not promise not to go," I reminded him. "I had to go, and I tell you now that I must go again, and again, until I see the Under-Water person and try to count *coup* upon him!"

The Dreadful River Cave

"No, no, my friend," Old Sun said to my father, interrupting another angry outburst he was about to make. "Be calm, my friend. Let us listen to the boy." And then to me: "Black Elk, my son, relate. Tell us all about your day."

There really was not much for me to tell. I said that the tracks we had found in the sand were no larger and no different from those of my own feet. I mentioned that many otters came upstream to fish in the pool at the foot of the falls, but that they seemed to have fear of the place and hurried off downstream with their catches of trout. I made no mention of the bears that I had seen.

"Well, what have you seen — the fresh footprints in the sand, and especially the actions of the otters — is very interesting. To me it is proof enough that the river cave is regularly inhabited by an Under-Water person," said Old Sun.

"And if by one, then probably by more, a family, perhaps even a clan of them!" my father cried. "And they have powerful medicine; there is no knowing how terribly powerful it may be. Black Elk, my son, I cannot bear to have you frequenting that place!"

"But they are people of the water. Only in the water have they killed or attempted to kill any of us land-dwellers. My friend, be reasonable. Allow your son to continue to watch for them at the pool. They cannot come out upon the land to attack him. Just think what a great *coup* he will count

We Watch Dreadful Cave

if he kills one of them!" Thus Old Sun to my father.

And he was silent for a long time, thinking hard. Imagine what was my suspense waiting for his words; and that of Dove Woman, sitting close beside me. She reached out for my hand and firmly gripped it as she stared at him. And at last he said:

"It is true, as you say, Old Sun, my friend, that the Under-Water People have done all their killing of our people in the water. More than that, until this discovery at the pool by our young ones, their tracks have never been seen on the shores of the rivers and lakes that they are known to inhabit. With old age one's heart gradually loses courage. It may be that I am too timid, too cautious. Well, much as I dread to let him do it, the boy shall have his way, and you and I must pray to the gods for his safety."

"He will survive the dangers. Something, my medicine, tells me that he is to make a great name for himself!" Old Sun exclaimed.

"And Dove Woman, I want her to be free to go with me. I can have no other companion, and well you know that four eyes, four ears, make for safety better than two," I said, looking straight across the lodge at old Red Wing Woman.

"Youth, you need n't stare so angrily at me!" she snapped. "If your father can allow you to continue watching for Under-Water evil people, I can risk my girl going with you!"

The Dreadful River Cave

"Oh, good, good! Oh, how generous of you! Oh, grandmother, how I love you!" Dove Woman cried.

"Ha! You mean that you are glad to get away from lodge work!" the old woman growled. But her eyes were soft and full of love as she looked across at the girl. And Dove Woman — she sprang from the couch and ran around the fireplace and knelt beside the old woman and hugged and kissed her.

"To-morrow we shall watch again for the Under-Water person," I said.

"Oh, no! To-morrow we plant the sacred seed; we need your help!" my father answered. And of course I was glad enough to give it.

Well, the great day broke with a cloudless sky. We had a very early meal and by the time we had finished eating, Old Sun and his family and Red Wing Woman and Dove Woman were seated in our lodge. My father was to conduct the ceremonies for the planting of the sacred seed because his was the Beaver medicine. Later on, when we should hear the first thunder of spring, Old Sun would unwrap his Thunder medicine, and we would help him pray for rains to make the young plants grow.

Very ancient was the Beaver medicine. In that long-ago time when the people and the animals could talk with one another, and the animals change into human form and back again at will, a young man named Spotted Robe left camp and traveled

40

We Watch Dreadful Cave

about seeking a powerful life-medicine. He was passing a cave in a cliff close to a river shore when he heard strange and beautiful singing within it. He turned and went to the cave and saw that it was a home of beavers. It was beautifully furnished with soft fur couches, and its walls were hung with rich garments of strange and wonderful design. At the back of the cave sat a very large, perfectly white beaver, and on either side of him, upon their couches, sat his wives and children; they were not white; all were of the natural beaver color.

When Spotted Robe appeared in the mouth of the cave the white beaver looked up and said to him: "Youth, I know why you are traveling about; I know what you seek. Enter and remain with us. I shall help you."

It was not without some fear in his heart that Spotted Robe accepted that invitation. But the beaver family, old and young, were so plainly glad to have him with them that his fears soon vanished and he remained with them all through the winter. The old white beaver was very close to Sun, maker of the days; Moon, his wife, Morning Star, their son; and Old Man, maker of the world. Because they loved him they had given him great intelligence and a most powerful medicine.

Spotted Robe had not been long there in the cave when the white beaver said to him one evening: "Well, my son, I see that you are of good character, honest and brave and kind-hearted, so I am

The Dreadful River Cave

going to teach you my medicine!" And teach him he did all through the long winter, all his prayers to the gods, all his sacred songs, and the dance and other ceremonies of the powerful medicine. And at last, when spring had come, and the young man was perfect in all these and was leaving for the camp of his people, he was given the emblem of the medicine, a beaver-gnawed, short length of a small birch-tree, and a sack of seeds of the beaver's sacred plant, nah-wak'-o-sis, the dried and crumbled leaves of which he put in a pipe and smoked to the gods when praying to them.

"I have told you how to plant these seeds," the white beaver said, "and with what prayers and ceremonies. Be sure to follow my instructions, else the seed will fail to grow to perfect leaf; and without the sacred smoke your prayers to the gods would be of no avail."

Spotted Robe cried when he parted from his kind beaver friends. He brought home the beaver medicine, planted the sacred seeds as he had been told to do, and had a fine growth of plants. He married and lived to great age, and when near death gave the medicine to one of his sons. And so from one to another it had been handed down through hundreds of winters, and now my father had it. During all that time it had been a very powerful medicine, bringing relief to the sick and success to those who went forth to war. Only recently had its power failed. And why? Because the

We Watch Dreadful Cave

old white beaver's instructions had been disobeyed! We all believed that with renewed planting and use of nah-wak'-o-sis its power would be renewed.

Said my father now, when we were all gathered in our lodge: "The earth is prepared and the sun is warming it. Let us pray the gods for their favor, and plant the sacred seeds!"

My mother sat on his left, Old Sun next to her, beyond him his women and children. I sat at the right of my father; next to me Red Wing Woman, then my almost-sister, after her my almost-mothers and their children.

The sacred medicine in its wrapping of four skins, a beaver, an otter, a loon, and a swan — all creatures of the water — was suspended from the lodge-poles above my father's couch. My mother took it down and laid it upon the ground in front of her. My father drew several coals from the fireplace with his red-painted willow tongs, and laid some dried sweetgrass upon them, and both he and my mother rubbed their hands in the perfumed smoke that arose from it, several times smoothing their bodies with handfuls of it, as to purify themselves for handling the sacred medicine. When they had done that, and my mother had untied the binding strings of the bundle, they began the first one of four water songs, the song of the beaver, during which they extended their hands over the bundle, and drew them back, and extended them, in time with the song; and then at the

The Dreadful River Cave

end of it my mother caressingly laid her hands upon the first of the wrappings, the tanned beaver-skin, and gently spread it open. In like manner the otter, the loon, and the swan songs were sung, and when the last wrapping, the swan-skin, was spread open, the medicine was revealed. First, there was a long pipestem, ornamented with bands of the fur of all the water animals, and with drooping plumes of the different water birds. On top of it was bound the stuffed skin of a water lizard. Beside the pipe-stem lay the length of birch-tree that the ancient beaver had given Spotted Robe, and three other beaver-gnawed sticks.

My father had previously filled a large stone pipe-bowl with nah-wak'-o-sis. He now reverently took up the sacred stem, fitted the bowl to it, lit the sacred filling with a coal from the fire, blew smoke to the sky, the ground, pointed the stem to the four world directions, and prayed: "Listen, O Sun! Listen, all you Above-People! Have pity upon us! Listen, Earth, our mother! Pity us! Listen, ancient beaver, you who gave us this medicine. Give us your help, and ask the gods to help us. We are about to plant seeds of the sacred nah-wak'-o-sis, your own medicine plant; we ask your help that the seeds may all take life and grow to perfect age. Protect the plants, O powerful ones, from grass-hoppers and all other eaters of leaves, and turn aside the steps of our enemies from this place. We now smoke to you, to all you gods of the sky, the

We Watch Dreadful Cave

air, and the earth, and the water. Men, women, children, we here and all the members of our three tribes, oh, pity us all! Give us all long life, and health, and happiness!"

He finished, and we all cried out: "Yes! Pity us, ancient beaver, and all you powerful gods!"

With both hands grasping the stem, my father passed the pipe to Old Sun, who received it with both hands, as only medicine men may do; all others are obliged to pass and to receive a pipe with one hand. Old Sun blew smoke as my father had done, and prayed as he had, except that he prayed also to his own medicine, the thunder bird. And then my father received back the pipe, and passed it on to me, and I took a few whiffs from it, cried out to the gods to have pity upon us all, and passed it back. And thus it went the round of the three of us until it was smoked out.

"I feel that the gods are pleased with the smoke that we have blown to them," said my father, "and that they have restored to us their favor. Let us proceed. Let us now sing the songs of the ancient beaver!"

Thereupon he handed to my mother the gnawed birch-stick, and to Old Sun's head wife, North Woman, and to Red Wing Woman, and to my almost-mother, Running Woman, he gave the three lesser beaver sticks, and they got upon their knees, put the sticks in their mouths, and placed their elbows close to the sides of their bodies, forearms

45

The Dreadful River Cave

up and hands drooping, appearing as much like sitting-up beavers as was possible. My father then began the first of the beaver songs, in which the rest of us joined, the four beaver women slightly raising and lowering their bodies and hands, and nodding their heads in time to the song, occasionally taking the sticks from their mouths and imitating the plaintive, almost childlike cry of a baby beaver. Very lively and heart-stirring were some of those songs, and some low and slow and sad. We sang them all, sixteen of them, and rested.

My father and Old Sun had painted themselves, their faces, hands, and moccasins, with red-earth paint, the sacred color, before the opening of the ceremony. My father now had me sit facing him and painted me, praying the ancient beaver and all the gods to look with favor upon me because I was to assist in the planting of the sacred seed. My mother then placed the sack of seed before him, and he refilled the pipe, lit it, and prayed long to the gods to put strong life into the seeds so that they would grow into large and perfect plants for our use. And so the ceremony ended. My mother rewrapped the medicine, hung it in place, and we all went out to the planting-place, my father, Old Sun, and I each taking a third of the seed in sacks of our own, and each a long, sharp-pointed, red-painted planting-stick. The women and children sat down on the east side of the planting-place. We three went to the southeast corner of it, faced the west,

We Watch Dreadful Cave

I on the left of my father and Old Sun on his right. We began the first of four planting-songs and each made a hole in the prepared earth with planting-stick, dropped into it a seed, and covered it. We then moved forward a short step and planted three more seeds. When we had each planted four seeds the first song was ended. We sang then the second of the songs, during which we each planted four more seeds, a short step apart. And so we went on planting and singing, across the place and back and forth, singing over and over again the four songs, and occasionally resting. During these rests the women and older children sang some of our songs, and one of their own, which was:

> " Seeds of nah-wak'-o-sis, grow! grow!
> Come up into the light.
> Seeds of nah-wak'-o-sis, grow! grow!
> Grow into large and perfect leaf!
> Grasshoppers, beware! Come not upon this
>   sacred ground!
> Sun, shine down; and Rain, do fall,
> And help these seeds to perfect life! "

Very soft and low and pleasant was this song of the women; it heartened us to arise and break into song and continue the planting of the seeds. And thus working and resting we went forth and back, forth and back, across the warm, soft earth, and the sun was low in the west when our work was completed, and we started toward our lodges, the women and children following us.

47

The Dreadful River Cave

We were about halfway to our little camp when there came from it a thunder-like roar of pain and anger, and through the doorway and bursting from under the sides of my father's lodge came that old chief bear and his wife and children. It was the chief bear who came through the doorway. He paused and sat up, still roaring, held up his left forepaw and licked it, his roar falling to a low whimpering, and then he roared again and went bounding away upon three legs, his woman and children trailing fast after him, and they passed out of our sight into the brush. Very, very thankful we were that they had not come our way, for we had not brought our weapons out to the planting-place; and even if we had had them, some of us must surely have been killed in the fight that would have taken place.

"Ha! That old sticky-mouth thief, he burned his foot in our fireplace! Come! Let us see what is left of our lodge! Oh, what shall I do if he has destroyed my sacred medicine!" my father cried.

We ran to the lodge, the women and children slowly and fearfully following, and went inside. It was in terrible condition: couches pulled apart, remains of our store of dried meat, dried berries, bladders of marrow grease and sacks of pemmican scattered about, the sacred medicine bundle pulled down, but unharmed. My father sprang forward and took it up and held it close in his arms. I looked at the fireplace. Before we left the lodge my mother

We Watch Dreadful Cave

had covered the bed of coals with a smooth, rounding layer of ashes, so that we should have fire upon our return. Well, deep into the center of the coalbed was the imprint of the chief bear's forepaw and smoke was rising from the exposed coals. There was no doubt that he had severely burned himself. I said as much to my father and Old Sun, and we laughed at the sudden shock of surprise and pain he must have had. But you may well believe that my mother and almost-mothers did not laugh when they came in and saw what the bears had done. They scolded us for being so light-hearted about it, and drove us out and told us not to return until they called us. We went over to Old Sun's lodge and his women gave us our evening meal. The bears had not entered his nor Red Wing Woman's lodge.

"My friends, this is by no means a happening for us to laugh at," said Old Sun after he had filled a pipe and passed it to my father to light. "That old sticky mouth will soon forget his burn, but he will not forget the feast that he has had here. Even if he should fear the place, his woman will coax him to come for more meat and grease and berries, and when they do come some of us will likely be killed."

"We have to remain here, so there is but one thing for us to do," said my father. "During the day we must keep a good watch out for them, and at night we must guard the camp by turns and be ever ready to start a fire in every lodge as soon as

The Dreadful River Cave

the guard hears them approaching and gives the alarm."

"Yes, that we must do," Old Sun agreed. "But not to-night. Right now that old sticky mouth has his burned paw in cool mud and will keep it there for some time to come."

"What a big one he is! I never saw one so large! I believe that it was he who killed Flying Elk, over on Cutbank River last summer," said my father.

"Just what I was thinking!" the other exclaimed. "And if it is he, then what chance would we three have against him? You remember that there were seven hunters with Flying Elk; that they all shot at the sticky mouth and wounded him, and that he charged and killed the poor man, and chased the others, all but killed two of them, and went off, apparently unhurt!"

I listened to all this, but said nothing. Right then I made my plan to attempt to kill the big bear. In this I could not ask my father and Old Sun to help me; they were medicine men, and could not fight a bear except in self-defense, because the bear, being himself of great medicine power, would break their medicine.

My father and I were presently called home and found our lodge again in good shape. He would not touch any of our food that the bears had pawed and mouthed over, fearing it might be bad medicine for him, so some was got for him from Red Wing Woman. He told me that I must go for fresh

We Watch Dreadful Cave

meat in the morning. I answered that I would do so, that I would have Dove Woman go with me; and then I asked him to lend the girl his gun. I had to plead with him for some time before he consented to do it.

We saddled the two horses and rode out of camp very early in the morning, Dove Woman patting and hugging my father's gun, and aiming it at rocks and trees and saying: "Bang! There, you are dead!"

"Be still! Get behind me and ride quietly and keep your eyes open, or else go back to camp and do lodge work!" I told her.

"Great chief, I live but to obey you," she laughed, and fell in behind me.

We rode to the top of the ridge from camp, then down along its crest through the last of the groves of pine and quaking aspens and looked out upon the great plains. In all directions as far as we could see they were black-patched with herds of buffaloes and antelopes, all quietly feeding or resting. Close ahead of us was a band of thirty or forty buffalo cows and calves, and yearlings and two-year-olds, just going into a sink in the ridge that contained a pond surrounded with a thick growth of willows. I waited until they had gone out of sight down the slope, then told the girl to remain where she was; that I would run the herd and kill a couple of the animals with my bow and arrows, which I also had with me.

The Dreadful River Cave

"But why have I a gun if I am not to use it? I want to run the herd with you!" she exclaimed.

"Keep still and do as I say. Hold my gun for me," I answered, and passed the weapon to her. "I had you carry my father's gun to-day just that you would become used to it. I shall soon be asking you to do something with it that you will fear to do."

"Say not fear to me! You will find me with you in anything that you attempt! And I think you are very mean not to let me make this run with you," she said as I rode on and drew my bow and strung it, and got a handful of arrows from the case.

I got almost upon the buffaloes before they discovered me, and in a short run dropped a yearling cow and a yearling bull, both fat and all the meat that I wanted. Dove Woman came up and I told her to help me butcher the animals as fast as she could, for we had other work to do before the setting of the sun. We were back in camp before noon with all the meat that our horses could carry, and after a short rest I called the girl and we set off afoot down the ridge, heading for the big beaver pond. I believed that the big bear and his family were in the swamp at the head of it, and would remain there until his burned foot healed. It was my intention to kill an elk or deer or moose near the pond, and then try to kill the bear when he came to feast upon it.

When we came to the big trail running by the pond we saw that the bear family had gone up it;

HE WENT SPLASHING AND STAGGERING THROUGH THE
SHALLOWS

We Watch Dreadful Cave

there was no mistaking their footprints. We followed along, but never stepped in it, and found where the bears had turned from it into the swamp just as I had believed they would. At that we back-trailed and went down through the brush and timber to the edge of the pond and looked out. It was as though the gods were directing our steps that afternoon: a bull moose was coming down toward us along the edge of the water and sometimes in it, stopping now and then to browse upon the tips of red willows, and the little wind there was came down the valley. I set my gun against a tree and stood ready for him with bow and arrows. On he came, suspecting no danger, and when he was about to pass, and no more than fifteen paces from where we stood, I sent an arrow fair into him just back of his shoulder. He snorted, whirled about, and got an arrow in his other side; and at that he went splashing and staggering through the shallows and fell dead upon the shore.

CHAPTER IV

A DAY WITH THE FOREST ANIMALS

WE lost no time in partially skinning the great animal, and taking out its insides, so that the meat would be exposed to the air and not soon spoil; and I cut out the tongue and hung it in a tree, sacrificing it to the sun and praying him to help us in our attempt to kill the old chief bear. Had I chosen the place for this I could not have done better; not far out from shore, no more than thirty or forty steps, was a large beaver lodge from the top of which we could watch for the bears to come to the meat; and to get to it with dry clothing and weapons we had to do no more than to make a skin boat. I thought that the skin of the moose would be large enough, so we entirely removed it from the carcass and cut some strips from along its edges for strings. We then made a circular, shallow frame of willows, like a great round dish, stretched the skin upon it, fastening it in place with the rawhide strings and plugging the two arrow holes, and the work was done. I then found a long, light pole for pushing the boat, and we set it afloat and carefully got into it. We saw at once that it was none too large; its round side was in places no more than the width of my hand above the water; we should have to keep it evenly balanced and propel it very slowly,

A Day with the Forest Animals

else it would fill and go down with us. We rode down to the dam in it, there fastened it to some bushes, and hurried homeward up the ridge in the gathering night, very well pleased with our work.

We were not now having any daytime lodge fires for fear that some enemy war party, looking out upon the country from the high places, would see the smoke. We arrived in camp just as the women were starting the evening fires. We saw Red Wing Woman going into my father's lodge, so Dove Woman came in there with me.

"Never was I so hungry! Roast at least three ribs of meat for me, and give me, too, a good portion of dried backfat," I told my mother.

She laughed and said that I could have six roasted ribs if I wanted them.

My father sent for Old Sun to join us in our evening meal, and when he had come in, and my father had filled and lighted a pipe, he asked what Dove Woman and I had been doing that afternoon. I had been waiting for that. I carefully explained all that we had accomplished toward putting an end to the wanderings of the old chief bear. No one interrupted me as I talked, but I could see my father and Old Sun now and then negatively shaking their heads, and Red Wing Woman fairly swelling with the words she would presently let loose at us. I had barely finished what I had to say when she cried:

"Bear Eagle! Old Sun! Heard you ever such

The Dreadful River Cave

crazy talk as this? The youth explains that in this plan of his to kill the old chief bear, my child and he will run no risk. No risk! And that beaver pond alive with Under-Water People eager to upset their little skin boat and drag them down to their death! No risk! And what, I should like to know, is to prevent that old bear, wounded and full of anger, and his wicked wife, from swimming out to that beaver lodge and tearing them and the lodge itself to mere shreds of flesh and scattered floating sticks?"

"But the old chief bear will not be merely wounded; at that close range I can surely put a bullet into his brain and drop him dead. As to his wife — well, should she swim out to attack us, there would be plenty of time for me to reload. I could not miss her head as she came swimming to the beaver lodge. And, too, Dove Woman would be right there beside me with my father's gun," I said.

My father stopped the old woman's further protests with raised hand. He turned to Old Sun and looked at him questioningly.

"Well, I will say this," he answered. "Provided they can go to and from the pond without being attacked, I believe that they will run very little risk. I really believe that they will kill that old sticky mouth. As to the Under-Water People, it is well known that they do not live in beaver ponds; they cannot camp upon soft mud bottoms."

"The timber is very scattering upon the slope

A Day with the Forest Animals

to the foot of the pond; should the bears be there we should see them from afar and turn back," I explained.

"My son," exclaimed my father, clapping his hands together with a loud smack, "maybe I am making the greatest mistake of my life, but I cannot do else than say to you: Go ahead, you and Dove Woman, with your plan! Old Sun and I will make medicine for you. We will pray the gods to give you success. We will make rich sacrifices to them. Surely, now that we are making them smoke offerings of the sacred nah-wak'-o-sis, as of old, they will listen to us."

Old Red Woman stared at my father as he said that, and gasped and stuttered, and finally managed to cry out: "Medicine man, do as you will with your son, but not with my grandchild, the only kin that I have left! The terrible dangers down at that beaver pond are not for her to risk."

"Woman, absolutely close your mouth![1] Be ashamed of yourself!" my father commanded her. "If my son, with your grandchild's help, can kill that old chief sticky mouth as he has planned to do, and with but little risk, is not that better than some of us being killed by him here at night in our lodges? Be brave! Go you home now and think how important is my son's undertaking. Remember that we are here for a most sacred purpose; one

[1] The Blackfeet is by no means a poor language. The above is an exact translation.

57

The Dreadful River Cave

upon which the very life of our people depends. Yes! Go and think about it; pray about it. If you will do that I feel sure you will come to me in the morning and say that, if I can permit my loved son to take a little risk for the good of us all, you can allow your girl to do the same."

"I do not need to go and think and pray about it," the old woman answered. "Always with your smooth talk and your reasons for this and for that you get the best of me. I give in. Dove Woman may go with your son or remain with me as she pleases."

"Oh, grandmother! Of course I choose to help my almost-brother kill the bear!" Dove Woman told her.

And so the matter was settled. But if Red Wing Woman's heart was as low as her tear-streaked face and trembling hands showed that it was, it was very low indeed. Her sadness was a shadow upon our evening meal.

Dove Woman and I did not go to the beaver pond on the following day, as my father and Old Sun advised that the bears should have time to find the moose carcass and feed upon it before we began our watch for them. We went instead to our resting-place behind the juniper brush and watched the falls and the wide, deep pool, our hearts strong with hope that we should this time see the Under-Water person who lived in the river cave in the cliff. Otters came to fish in the pool, as usual, and

A Day with the Forest Animals

swam off downstream with their prey. Late in the afternoon two beavers, evidently a two-year-old male and his wife, came upstream into the pool, swam around and around in it, landed in several places and explored the shore, and then attempted to climb the falls. The larger one of them, the male, leading, they went up along the edge of the rock on the right of the falls until they reached the first shelf, and then slipped into the water and were swept down into the depths at the foot of it. When they came up they swam to the shore on the left side of the pool and sat up side by side, and for a long time stared at the falls, occasionally leaning together and rubbing noses. They were, of course, a young new-married pair that had been told by the chief of their clan, somewhere below, to strike out and make a home of their own. Every spring there were many such departures from every beaver pond. That had to be else the steady increase in the numbers of the clan would soon eat out all the food growths along the shores of the pond and the whole clan would be obliged to move and build a new dam and new houses. The young couple at last decided to try to ascend the left side of the falls, and again they reached the first shelf, and were faced by an unclimbable face of rock; so into the water they went, and for all their desperate struggles were swept back into the pool. They came ashore this time upon the little sandy point where we had found the footprints of the Under-Water

The Dreadful River Cave

person. There they rested for a time and then moved out through the little patch of brush and began climbing the very steep, rocky slope of the cañon; and there, about halfway up to our level, a straight-up rise of the rock barred their way. Right there they gave up all hope of surmounting the rise, and waddled and slid back to the water and swam off downstream.

There were, as I well knew, several clans of beavers living along the two streams running into the lake above the falls, and still another clan at the foot of the lake. But no young new-mated couple had been the founders of those clans. An old and very wise beaver had led the first migration to the upper part of the valley, and finding that he could not ascend the falls nor the rocky slope of the cañon, he had turned back downstream to the head of the swamp, and struck out upon a well-beaten game trail that went through the timber and up a steep but unbroken slope away to the left of the cañon, and thence by easy descent to the foot of the lower lake. My son, themselves defenseless, what wonderful courage beavers must have to go out far from the water along trails running through heavy timber and brush that they know is inhabited by mountain lions, lynxes, wolves, coyotes, wolverines, and fishes, and other enemies! I have often thought of that. And I have another thought about it, too: it may be that the beavers are very much nearer the gods than we are; it may be that

A Day with the Forest Animals

the gods tell them where to go, and then remove all dangers from their trails.

Well, though we remained at our watching-place until near sundown we did not see the Under-Water person. We would have liked to remain there until night, but that was more than we dared do: the thought of meeting that old chief bear and his wife in the dark timber hurried our homeward steps. We had little to report to our people that evening. It was decided that we should go to the beaver pond and watch for the bears on the following day, and before bedtime my father and Old Sun gave us many instructions as to just what we were and were not to do.

As all animals, grass-eaters and meat-eaters alike, generally do very little moving about during the middle of the day, especially in the summer-time, we did not leave camp until the sun was shining almost straight down through the smoke-hole of our lodge. We went down the ridge to the head of the lake, and then very slowly and watchfully up through the scattering timber to the beaver dam, where we found our skin boat just as we had left it. We got in, taking with us a couple of arm-fuls of willow brush, and I very slowly poled out toward the beaver lodge in front of the moose carcass. Before we arrived there we could see that something had been at the meat, and upon nearer approach discovered that the carcass was almost half eaten. I poled on more slowly; so slowly that

61

The Dreadful River Cave

we seemed hardly to move, and after a long time
we touched the outer edge of the beaver lodge.
Dove Woman got out upon it first, crawling slowly
from the boat, and after passing her the weapons
and the brush I fastened the boat to a projecting
stick of the lodge and crawled out beside her. Then,
with the least possible and very slow movement,
we set up the brush for a screen in front of us. From
this height above the water we could plainly see
what remained of the big moose carcass. The upper
ham was eaten to the bone, and there was a large
hole in the one that lay upon the ground. All the
ribs had been gnawed or torn from the backbone.
The neck and head were as yet untouched. The tall
grass around the carcass had been flattened to the
ground by the tread of heavy feet.

The top of that beaver lodge was an uncomfort-
able resting-place; we could not sit up, for if we did
we should be head and shoulders above the brush;
we were obliged to lie flat behind it, and the un-
evenly laid sticks with which it was constructed
pressed somewhat painfully into our flesh. Close
under us the construction was, of course, of sticks
closely, solidly packed with mud, excepting a cen-
tral, narrow space which provided fresh air for the
occupants of the lodge. By pressing our faces close
above this opening we could feel the warm air coming up through it, and smell the musky odor of the
beavers. Now and then we could hear the faint,
baby-like whimpers of young ones as they nosed

A Day with the Forest Animals

their mother and crowded one another to get at her milk. The entrances to the two or three passageways leading up to the living-place were well down to the bottom of the lodge, which stood in water almost twice as deep as the length of my body. The floor of the living-place, as you well know, was above the surface of the pond. The mother beaver and her mate, and no doubt several yearling children still living with them, had already begun collecting their store of winter food; upon the bottom of the pond, close at each side of the lodge, were piles of fresh cuttings of quaking aspens, cottonwoods, willows, and small birch. How very wise are the beavers! No matter how long and cold the winter, and thick the ice, they never want for food. Whenever they are hungry they swim out to a pile of their sticks, drag one up into the entrance to the lodge and eat the bark, and then take the bare stick out to a refuse-pile.

Well, we had not been long upon the beaver lodge when three coyotes came from the timber and brush out to the carcass. Evidently they had been to it not long before, for they seemed not to be hungry; they nosed the meat here and there, licked it, took only an occasional small bite of it, and then came to the shore of the pond and had a few laps of water, just for something to do, for they were no more thirsty than they were hungry. All three were old males. Their new growth of summer hair was pushing off their heavy winter growth, and it

The Dreadful River Cave

hung upon them in faded, ragged patches; they
were very shabby. They went from the water back
to the carcass and gave it a few more licks, acting
as though they were mad at themselves because
their stomachs could hold no more of the good
meat. But they were not going to leave it; they
went to the edge of the brush and lay down. One
of them kept his head up and his eyes open; the
others went to sleep.

Came now numbers of the three kinds of meat
birds that live in the timber, more and more until
there was a crowd of them fluttering and quarreling over the carcass, crowding one another away
from the most tender parts of the meat. The noise
that they made was not pleasing to our ears; it was
so loud that it echoed all about us. I whispered to
my almost-sister that it would attract other meat-
eaters to the carcass.

And sure enough, a big-headed, short-faced wolverine soon came trotting out from the brush and
began to tear at the meat with hoarse growls and
snufflings. The birds flew up into near branches
of the trees and scolded down at him. The coyote
upon watch aroused the others and they made a
rush at him as though they were going to tear him
to pieces. But when they were almost upon him he
whirled about with bared teeth and wrinkled snout
and angry growl, and all three leaped back to a safe
distance from him. He growled two or three times
more at them, then turned back to the carcass and

resumed his feasting. They looked at one another, took courage and advanced, and again he whirled about and they retreated, and stood as before, pretending to take no notice of him, but watching his every movement, their anger increasing with every mouthful he tore from what they considered their own find of food. But what could they do? Nothing. He would not run from them and they dared not attack him. They raised their sharp noses to the sky and shrilly yelped their hurt feelings to all the listening creatures of the valley.

A passing cougar heard them, and the scolding meat birds, and came to learn what the trouble was. He had no more than stuck his head out from the brush than the coyotes went one way, the wolverine another, and were gone from there as quick as a flash of lightning. The cougar stared after them, listened to the pattering of their feet, and then slowly walked out to the carcass, his long tail swaying and jerking with all the motions of a dying snake. When he came to the carcass he stopped and looked about in all directions, even out toward us. Fierce enough was the glare of his big yellow eyes, but well we knew that they lied, that in his heart was great fear of man.

Having satisfied himself that there were no enemies about — the little summer wind was from him to us — he lowered his head and smelled of the meat; moved on and smelled it all along from head to the end of the hind legs. But he ate none of it,

The Dreadful River Cave

nor even licked it. Cougars seldom eat meat that they find: they seem to prefer to kill their food, and that they do easily enough. With noiseless feet they sneak close to a deer or elk or moose, and spring upon his shoulders, and with one snap of their long-tusked jaws, or a sudden twist with their sharp-clawed forefeet, break his neck. But although this cougar did not want any of this meat, he somehow seemed to think that he might want it at some future time, and so he began to cover it with what material he could find, dead sticks, fallen branches, and pawings of dead grass.

Dove Woman nudged me; we looked at one another and smiled, and she whispered: "What a funny, foolish thing he is doing!"

"Yes. Just you wait until the bears appear and you will see that covering flying in all directions," I answered.

The cougar must have faintly heard me. Anyhow, he paused and stared out in our direction a long time, and jerked his head as he sniffed the air. Then he suddenly turned and stared into the brush upshore from the carcass, and we did, too, for we heard a dry stick snap, and then another. Presently we saw the brush shake as some large animal advanced through it, and at last out from it came a big bear followed by her young ones, three of them. There was no mistaking her: she was the wife of the old chief bear! As she advanced toward the carcass, the cougar, on the other side of it, backed away.

A Day with the Forest Animals

She did not at first see him, but when she discovered him sneaking away all her hair bristled forward, and with humped back and angry growls she stiffly sidled toward him and made but a few steps when he leaped into the brush and was gone. She stopped short and stared at the place of his disappearance, sniffed the air, became sure that he had really gone, and turned back to the carcass, her hair gradually settling back into place.

Frightened by their mother's angry growls, the three young had kept close to her heels. They now began to play about the carcass, and she to tear mouthfuls of meat from the lower hind leg, after tossing one way and another the sticks and brush that partly concealed it. All this time I had paid no attention to Dove Woman. I now looked at her; she was staring at the bear with wrinkled brows and tight-closed lips, her hands hard gripping my father's gun.

I leaned closer to her and whispered: "Are you afraid?"

"No! But why don't you hurry and take good aim and shoot her?" she answered.

"Old chief bear, he is the one we most want; after we kill him we will try to kill his wife. Be patient! I think that we shall soon see him," I told her.

And anyhow I could not have killed the bear as she stood, head from me. I did not intend to fire at her, nor any other bear, unless I could get a good aim at the head just below the back of the ear.

The Dreadful River Cave

Came now five wolves trotting along the shore from the direction of the dam, and at once I knew why so much of the big moose carcass had been eaten in so short a time; they had been feasting upon it as well as the bears. They came steadily on, looking neither to the right nor left, intent only upon going straight to the meat. An old, faded gray-white male was in the lead. I whispered to Dove Woman: "What a surprise those wolves are going to get when they pass that patch of red willows!"

The willows thickly covered a little outstretching point of the shore, not more than three or four steps from where the bear stood, still feasting upon the carcass. Her young ones were playing tag, just as our children do, two of them chasing the other around and around the flattened grass and shore where the carcass lay. And now, just as the old lead wolf was close to the willows, the chased young one made a rush through them and right against his legs, and he was so startled that he leaped high to one side and splashed down into the edge of the pond. The young one stumbled and rolled over when it ran against the wolf, and at the same time getting the scent of the wolf enemy it squalled loudly for its mother. The wolf next in line had whirled about against the others when the leader sprang so suddenly out into the water, and now it and the old leader too made a rush at the young one, upon its feet and running for the brush, and the three other wolves closely followed them.

A Day with the Forest Animals

The second wolf of the line was now nearest the bear child and made a lunge at it as it rushed into the brush, and would have surely caught it had not the old lead wolf, leaping in from the shore, run into him, almost knocking him down. The old leader did not pause; he darted into the brush after the little one, eager for this revenge upon the whole bear tribe that had so often driven him and his followers from their kills of good meat, buffalo, elk, deer, antelope, moose, and other grass-eaters, and all unsuspicious of what was coming to him.

As quickly as I can clap my hands together, old mother bear whirled about from her feasting when she heard her young one cry for help, saw her two other young, terribly frightened, running toward her from the point of brush, and so knew what way to go. She made a long leap and passed over the two young ones; another leap and struck the ground at the edge of the willows; a third leap — high above the brush and then down into it and right onto that old lead wolf! She gave a thunder-like roar as she struck him. We heard crunching of bones. And then from the swamp at the head of the pond, there came to our ears another thunder-like bear roar, a roar so loud, so long, so deep that it made us shiver! None but the old chief bear could have roared like that.

"He comes!" I heard Dove Woman exclaim in a hard-breathed whisper.

"Yes! Take courage!" I told her, but never took my eyes off the patch of brush.

CHAPTER V

WE DISCOVER AN ENEMY

I COULD not see the mother bear as she bit into that old chief wolf. His followers were gone; all had fled into the timber when she roared. She now came out of the brush with the neck of the wolf in her jaws, and dropped him near the moose carcass and furiously bit into his back from head to tail, and crunched the head again and again until it was a shapeless mass of torn skin and broken bones. Before she came out of the brush her three young had been running and squalling about upon the flattened grass, almost crazy with fear, knowing not what to do. But when she appeared they ran toward her, then saw the wolf dangling from her mouth and ran back past the moose carcass to the edge of the brush and sat up in a row, sniffing the air with their little black, wrinkled noses, looking at one another, and then out at her. At last she turned away from the wolf and they ran to her and closely followed her to the water's edge, where she drank thirstily, and then waded out a little way and lay down, only her head remaining above the water. And at that the young ones waded and swam out and got upon her back, crowding closely together.

And then we heard what we had been listening

We Discover an Enemy

for, the approach of the old chief bear. Off in the timber a dry stick snapped; then another. The mother bear heard the snapping, too, and stood up and looked off in the direction from which the sounds came, her young sliding into the water and making their way back to shore. She sat up when still another stick snapped, and sniffed the air. The wind was toward her from the timber; she made sure that the odor she got was that of her mate and waded ashore and went on into the timber to meet him, her young close following.

"Ha! We shall soon see the old chief bear! He will soon be out there feasting upon the carcass," I whispered to my almost-sister.

"Oh, I am afraid! That old wife of his crunching the bones of the wolf! What anger was in her heart! What terrible anger!" she said.

"Fear not! Just pray the gods to help us," I told her.

I said that very calmly, but I was not calm inside of me; my heart was beating so hard and fast that I could feel the throb of it away up in my throat. I watched the brush along the shore and back of the carcass, but nowhere could I see it quiver. There was no more snapping of dry sticks back in the timber. A big beaver came to the surface of the pond just behind us, saw us lying upon his lodge, and the loud slap of his tail as he dived made us almost spring to our knees. Time passed. The meat birds were all back upon the carcass,

The Dreadful River Cave

fluttering about upon it and scolding and fighting for the best places. More and more time passed and neither the bears nor any other animals came in sight.

Said Dove Woman, at last: "Perhaps it was not the old chief bear that did the stick-snapping over there in the timber."

"Just what I was thinking. It may have been a passing elk or some other grass-eater," I answered.

The sun was now about to trail down behind the mountains and still we lingered there, but with less and less hope of seeing the bears. And then, when the sun went behind the great bare peak in front of us, we knew that we had to go if we were to get home before dark. We got into the boat and I poled it toward the dam. Dove Woman sat facing me. When we were near our landing-place she suddenly straightened up and gasped: "Look! The bears! There at the moose carcass!"

I turned about so suddenly that I almost upset the boat; some water did come in over the edge before we could balance it. Yes, sure enough, there were the bears, the old chief bear, his wife and children, coming down the shore of the pond toward the carcass, the old chief last and limping along upon three legs! In going over a log he slipped, his sore foot struck the ground, and he let out a terrible roar, just such a roar as we had heard echoing out from the swamp. Perhaps that, too, had been a roar of pain, and not, as we had thought, his an-

We Discover an Enemy

swer to his wife's roar of anger when she sprang
upon the wolf. I dared not use my pole. There was
a faint evening breeze and we drifted with it, not
toward the dam, but toward the east shore of the
pond. The bears did not see us; they did not once
look out our way. Long before we landed they were
feasting upon the carcass. Night had come by the
time we finally tied the boat to the brush and made
our way to the dam. We crossed upon it slowly and
noiselessly, and as soon as we were a little way up
the slope of the ridge, we started running and kept
running until we arrived in camp.

There was a light only in my father's lodge. As
we neared it we could hear no talking, no sound of
life inside, and did not know what to make of it. I
whispered to Dove Woman that we would sneak to
the lodge and peek in. We did so, and saw the people, even the children, sitting all bowed over and
staring mournfully at the fire.

"Ha! What is the trouble here?" I asked, as I
thrust aside the door curtain and stepped inside
close followed by the girl.

Then with what cries of joy were we welcomed:
"You survive!" "You are returned!" "The gods
are good to us!" the women cried.

I turned to my smiling father: "What is it all
about?" I asked him.

"Why, some time back, at sun-went-down, we
heard a thunder-like sticky mouth's roar away
down there in the valley. We waited and waited

73

The Dreadful River Cave

and you did not come! We feared that you both had been killed!" he explained.

"I did n't! I kept telling them that our medicine was strong, that you would surely return to us," said Old Sun.

"Had they been your very own children, why, perhaps you would not have been so certain about it," old Red Wing Woman told him. The old man did not answer her.

"You saw the sticky-mouth chief? You heard him roar?" my father asked.

"We did! We did! And saw his old wife make a wolf-killing! Oh, her anger was something terrible; it made me shiver!" Dove Woman cried.

And as she had begun, I let her relate all that we had seen at the pond, the while we ate the food that the women set before us. My father and Old Sun alone laughed when she told how the old chief bear had limped along the shore, holding his burned foot well up in front of him, and how he had roared when he slipped down upon it. The women kept exclaiming, "Oh! Oh! How terrible!" The children were so frightened by what they heard that they crept into their mothers' laps, crying, some of them.

Old Red Wing Woman scowled and groaned more and more as the tale went on, and when it was ended she cried out: "There! You see now, you medicine men, into what terrible danger you are forcing my daughter. My only child, all that I have to be company to me in my old age!"

We Discover an Enemy

"I don't see that she was in any great danger," said Old Sun.

"I was n't!" Dove Woman cried. "Oh! Oh! This has been the most wonderful — the most interesting day of my life!"

"Ha! Crazy! That is what she is, just wholly crazy!" the old woman muttered.

Came another cloudless, warm day. Dove Woman and I remained in camp until noon, and before we started for the beaver pond my father and Old Sun painted us with sacred red, and prayed the gods to give us success in our undertaking. On our way down the ridge we saw several deer and elk, and when near the pond a lone old buffalo bull. He neither saw nor heard us, as we sneaked around him to the dam and across it, and up the shore to our boat. There was considerable water in the boat. We emptied it out and got in and started off across the pond. Not an animal of any kind was in sight, nor could we see the moose carcass upon the farther shore. Upon approaching the beaver lodge upon which we had lain, we discovered that the willow brush we had taken there was gone, every branch of it; during the night the beavers for some reason or other had removed it. And then, looking from the lodge across to the shore, we saw that what had been left of the carcass was gone, too; not even a single gnawed bone of it remaining upon the hard-trampled patch of grass.

The Dreadful River Cave

"What can have become of it?" Dove Woman signed to me.

"The bears—maybe the wolves—have dragged it off into the timber," I answered, and slowly poled the boat on to the shore and stepped out, telling the girl to remain where she was. But she would not do that. She got out, too, drew the boat half out of the water, and followed me to the edge of the brush. It was very thick. I did not like to go into it, but felt that I must. I had to find the remains of the carcass and bring it back into the open where it had lain. We found where the animals had gone off with it and followed the trail some little distance into the timber and saw that there was no longer any carcass. It had been torn apart; all that was left of it was the clean gnawed head, and a bone here and there stripped of every shred of meat. That was a great disappointment!

I signed the girl to turn back to the shore and followed her. If we were to continue our quest of the old chief bear we had to kill another big meat animal for him to feed upon. There was the old buffalo bull, close by in the timber. I decided that he would be of no use to us where he was. What we needed was another carcass right here upon the shore of the pond. True, we might kill him and bring his body here piece by piece, but the pieces would be so small and light that the meat-eaters would carry them off into the brush to devour them.

We Discover an Enemy

We got back into the boat, and as I poled it out toward the beaver lodge I told Dove Woman what was troubling me.

"Almost-brother," she said, after some thought, "if we kill the bull it will not be necessary to bring his meat here; the bears will soon find his carcass. And listen! We can build a resting-place in a tree from which to watch for the bears, and be more safe from attack by them than we were here upon this beaver lodge. We shall be absolutely safe from them because, as all the hunters say, these real bears cannot climb trees."

"Almost-sister!" I cried — yes, right out loud so that my words echoed out across the pond and into the timber — "I marvel at your wisdom! When the gods saw what you were they put into your woman body the wisdom of a great chief! What you propose is good; it is an almost perfect plan. The one risk we will run is the getting to and from our tree watching-place, but we must take that chance. Come! Let us go find the bull!"

Down through the many winters and summers of my life has always been with me the memory of my almost-sister's happy, smiling face as she heard my all too few words of praise. She said nothing, just smiled, and in her big brown eyes was a strange, far-away look as though she could actually see, there in the clear, strong light of day, the things that are given us to see only in our shadow visions in the darkness of the night.

The Dreadful River Cave

We went on down to the dam, tied our boat to the brush and took our back trail, and, presently, the trail of the bull. He had gone on some distance from where we had seen him, and, when we sighted him, was approaching the swamp at the head of the beaver pond. But he was busily feeding upon the grass and vines growing here and there between the patches of brush, his head down the most of the time, so we had no difficulty in closely approaching him upon his down-wind side. I had not my bow and arrows with me, so I signed to my almost-sister to do the shooting. She rested her gun against the side of a tree and took long and careful aim. Boom! The bull flinched, threw up his head and humped his back, made two or three forward leaps, staggered and fell heavily upon his side, and with a few gasps was dead.

This time my almost-sister was not so excited over her kill, yet she was pleased enough at the accuracy of her aim. While she was examining the big animal I reloaded her gun, meantime looking at the surrounding trees. I had the choice of three wide-branching cottonwoods between which the bull had fallen, and chose the one on the down-wind — the east side of the animal, and no more than thirty steps from it.

"Come! Let us do what we have to do as quickly as we can," I told Dove Woman. We first propped the bull upon his back and skinned down the hide to the ground upon both sides. We then took out

We Discover an Enemy

the insides, and cut a piece of the hide into long, stout strings. And always, while we worked, we kept a sharp lookout in the direction of the swamp; well we knew what risk we were taking: the old chief bear was certainly somewhere there in the swamp, and might come out upon us at any time.

We now brought to the foot of the tree a number of dry, fallen poles which we found in a near-by thicket of pines. I then climbed up into the tree and the girl passed up to me the rawhide strings, and the poles as fast as I could lay and bind them, and we soon had a long, wide platform securely resting upon two stout branches of the tree, and high enough to be beyond reach of any mad bear's claws. To make it a really comfortable watching-place, I spread upon it a couple of armfuls of balsam branches which I had the girl gather for me. And then, sliding down from the tree, I fastened the liver and lungs to a length of rawhide string, and the girl following me with our guns, dragged them down through the timber to the place where the moose carcass had lain on the shore of the pond. I believed that the bears would come there in hope of finding a few last pickings of meat, and if they did they would find the drag, and follow the trail of it straight to our new kill. "This time," I told the girl as we hurried home, "we cannot fail to kill the old bear chief!"

And so thought my father and Old Sun when we explained to them what we had done.

The Dreadful River Cave

On the following day Dove Woman and I had to go out again for meat. It seemed that we never should get time to do the things that we wanted to do. We wanted to go to our platform in the tree and watch for the bears; we wanted to spend the latter part of each day at the falls, watching for the Under-Water person to come out of the cave in the cliff. We wanted, too, to go on discovery up in the valley beyond the falls, especially to the upper lake, and learn if any of our mountain enemies were there. It was one of their favorite camping places when they were sneaking about hunting upon our side of the range. If some of them were there, then were we likely to be discovered and attacked by them. Truly, it was a heavy load that my father and Old Sun had put upon us, the very life of our little camp!

On this morning I again carried my bow and arrows as well as my gun. Our horses, kept so steadily upon their picket ropes, were eager to go. At first we could not hold them in, could only guide them, so we headed from camp straight up the ridge, and the steep climb soon tamed them. Having them then well in hand we turned to the east along the slope of the ridge, riding slowly and keeping a good lookout for game. We were almost to the outer edge of the timber and about straight up from the foot of the lake, when, upon passing through a very thick stand of low pines surrounding a spring, I thought I smelled a faint odor of

We Discover an Enemy

smoke. I was not sure. I was bending close over my horse to avoid some low tree branches; but when I straightened up I found myself in front of a large, newly made war lodge, and could see another one beyond it. No perceptible smoke was rising from either of them, nor could I hear any talking. Dove Woman rode up beside me and stared at them. We saw a squirrel run into the near one through the curtainless doorway, and soon come out with a morsel of some kind of food in its mouth — probably dried meat — which was proof enough that the place was deserted. But for all that we got down from our horses with no little fear and hesitation, holding our guns ready and looking carefully in all directions as we moved slowly forward to the doorway of the first lodge and looked within. It was well and closely built of dead poles, with an outer layer of pieces of rotten logs, strips of bark, brush, moss, anything that would lie up against the poles and prevent the light of the fire from shining through. All around the inside of the lodge were smooth-laid couches of balsam boughs upon which the occupants had taken their one night's rest. I counted them: fourteen men had slept there. I handed the lead rope of my horse to Dove Woman and went inside, felt of the fireplace and found a still hot bed of coals beneath the ashes. And then between two of the brush beds I found a pair of worn-out moccasins that were embroidered with colored porcupine

The Dreadful River Cave

quills. The pattern was two fingers wide from the toes straight up the center to the tongues, and upon each side of them was a solidly embroidered circle, one red-colored, the other yellow, symbols of the sun and moon, we thought. It was an enemy pattern, not a pattern of any of our tribes, but what enemy we could not tell. We went on to the other lodge, which we found was some larger, and contained twenty beds. I let Dove Woman look about in it while I stood watch, and she came running out to me with a beautifully painted and fringed war case of parfleche which she had found under the head of one of the brush beds. We unlaced its top cover and drew out a splendid bonnet of eagle tail feathers, and then a fur and scalp-trimmed war shirt of very thin and well-tanned buckskin. Nor was that all; from the bottom of the case the girl brought out a red-painted buckskin sack, and we found that it contained a tanned and stuffed and feather-trimmed mink-skin, to the back of which was fastened a stuffed lizard no longer than my finger. A lizard different from any that we had ever seen; its skin was rainbow-colored.

It did not seem possible that the owner of these valuable garments, and the stuffed mink and lizard, his sacred medicines, could have forgotten that he had placed the case containing them under his brush pillow, and thoughtlessly gone off without it. No warrior would think of going upon a raid without his medicine.

We Discover an Enemy

"The man must have gone crazy, else he would have taken the case with him," I said.

"Is it not more likely that he turned coward, and left it here for an excuse to leave his party and return home?" said the girl.

"How wisely suspicious you are!" I answered. "And I believe that you are right. Warriors do not hide their medicine garments and skins under their beds; they keep the case containing them ready at hand with their weapons. There is no telling when the man will pretend to have just discovered his loss; maybe not until to-night; or he may now be on his way back. Just you stand here while I learn whence the enemy came and whither they went."

I circled out around the thick growth of pines and found their trail coming into it from straight down the valley, and going out of it straight to the north; and by that I thought that they were none of our across-the-mountains enemies; that they were most likely from one of our southern or eastern plains enemy tribes, Crows, or Sioux, or Spotted Horses People,[1] and traveling northward in the expectation of finding and raiding a camp of one of our tribes. I said to myself that the gods were surely protecting us: the enemy must have been down in the valley, or here putting up the war lodges, when we shot the buffalo bull, but they could not have heard the boom of the gun, else

[1] The Cheyennes.

83

The Dreadful River Cave

they would have come up into the valley to investigate. Had they done that, they possibly might be right now carrying our scalps! The latter was not a pleasant thought!

I returned to Dove Woman, told her what I had learned, and that we would do no hunting that day; that the one thing for us to do was to watch for the return of the enemy. Whether the man had purposely or thoughtlessly left his medicine in the lodge, I was sure that he would soon be coming back to it.

We remounted our horses and followed the trail of the war party to the top of the ridge and a little way down the north slope to the edge of the timber. Below, and separated from us by a strip of prairie running westward to the foot of the first mountain of the range, lay the narrow and thickly brushed valley of the south fork of Cutbank River. The trail of the enemy went straight down across that prairie strip, and I believed that the lone warrior would risk coming back across it in preference to traveling away around the head of it through the timber. We tied our horses well back from the prairie and then went out to the edge of it and sat down to watch for the man's appearance.

There were no buffaloes nor antelopes upon this narrow strip of prairie, but off to the east, where it merged into the great plain, were several small bands of antelopes, and beyond them was a very large herd of buffaloes. The nearest band of the

We Discover an Enemy

antelopes was slowly grazing up into the open strip and toward us.

Having nothing else to do, we opened the parfleche case and drew out the enemy's medicines and closely examined them. Never had I seen so beautiful a war bonnet. I set it upon my head and stood up and found that the tail of it actually touched the ground at my heels. Every feather of it was perfect, white-tipped, and banded at the base with a narrow strip of porcupine-quill embroidery in colors, and each side of the headband was fringed with six skins of the white weasel. Laying aside the bonnet, I put on the war shirt and found it to be a good fit. I set the bonnet back upon my head, took my small mirror from my side pouch, and admired myself.

"Almost-sister," I said, "if we could see that lone enemy coming up across this strip of prairie in front of us, I would go out to attack him dressed just as I am. Just think how surprised he would be when he found himself facing an enemy wearing his own war clothes!"

"Why talk so crazily?" she exclaimed. "Of course you wouldn't do it! You wouldn't think of wearing a man's own medicine when going out to fight him!"

"Of course I would!" I told her. "As he hid it away in order to have an excuse to desert his party, as he certainly has proved to be a coward, his medicine will no longer protect him. How can it protect

The Dreadful River Cave

him when I have it? I shall wear it, stuffed mink and lizard and all, while we remain here!" And with that I fastened the skins to the tail of the war bonnet.

Dove Woman said no more about it, but, oh, how reproachfully, sadly, she looked at me, not once but many times.

What a long day that was to us, sitting there watching for what we were, perhaps, never to see. We talked of the thing that we would rather be doing, watching for the old chief bear and his wife. We had to put an end to them before we could resume our watch of the falls for the Under-Water person.

Late in the afternoon the girl said to me: "Almost-brother, do listen to me; do please me: take off those enemy war clothes!"

"It is impossible for me to take your words," I answered. "Having said that I would wear them while I remain here, I must do so. Well you know that bad luck comes to those who turn about from what they have said they will do!"

She made no answer to that. I was smoothing out the arm fringe of the war shirt. I looked up at her to learn how she had taken my straight talk, and saw that she was staring intently down the slope. I looked that way: the lone warrior that I was now only half-expecting to see had come out of the brush bordering the little stream and was hurrying straight toward us!

CHAPTER VI

I GIVE MY ENEMY HIS LIFE

HA! There he is!" I exclaimed, and turned about upon hands and knees, crept back a little way into the timber, and then got up and ran to our horses. Dove Woman had closely followed me; she untied and mounted her animal as quickly as I did mine.

"You must not follow me into the open! Come no farther than the edge of the timber!" I told her.

She did not answer.

"You heard me?" I asked.

"I am not deaf!" she said.

I sat watching the enemy, whom I could indistinctly see through the tops of the brush. I waited until he was more than halfway up across the strip of prairie and then rode out at him. He saw me the instant I left the timber, stopped short, turned as though to run back to the brush, saw that I would be upon him before he could reach its shelter, and turned again and faced me as he fitted one of a handful of arrows to his bow. And now, finding that he had to fight, he proved to be no coward: he ran toward me, dodging from side to side to make more difficult my aim at him. As I rode nearer to him I saw that he was just a youth like myself, but

The Dreadful River Cave

of more slender build. That somehow surprised me. I had been picturing the lone enemy as a big, fierce-appearing man, a man of long experience in war.

"I will take a chance: he shall shoot first," I said to myself. And just then I heard a horse coming behind me, looked back, and saw that the rider was my almost-sister! And I had told her not to follow me!

"Turn back! Turn back!" I shouted to her.

I had not time to see if she obeyed me. I was getting close to my enemy. He had raised the war song of his people, a song strange to my ears. From looking back at the girl I turned and faced him just as he fired his arrow. It passed in front of me. He was fitting another arrow to his bow when he suddenly broke his war song and flinched back, and I knew that he had recognized his war clothes. I was already aiming my gun at him. I fired. Boom! His raised bow arm broke above the elbow and swung down uselessly, and the bow dropped from his hand. I saw no more of him just then, for my excited horse was trying to run away with me. I had to use all my strength to check his speed and turn him, and when I had done that and was giving all my attention to the reloading of my gun, there was Dove Woman heading me off and crying: "No! No! You shall not kill him! He is only a youth! You have broken his arm! Have pity on him, almost-brother! Let him live!"

"No! No! Get out of my way!" I shouted. I fin-

I Give my Enemy His Life

ished reloading and looked past her at my enemy. He was holding his knife out with his sound right hand. As I forced my way past Dove Woman he again raised his war song, but not loud as before, and then he staggered, the knife dropped from his hand, and he sank to the ground and lay motionless flat upon his back.

"Oh, almost-brother! See now how poor he is; how helpless! Surely you will let him live!" Dove Woman begged me.

"Well, as you plead so hard, I give you his life; he shall live if his wound does not kill him," I told her. But I hid from her what was really in my heart: my sudden great pity for the youth.

We rode up beside him and dismounted. I picked up his knife and stuck it inside of my belt. Dove Woman knelt beside him, felt of his broken arm, took out her knife and cut off the blood-soaked sleeve of his shirt; the wound, right through the big muscle of the upper arm, was bleeding fast. She cut a long strip from her leather robe, and had me bring her some straight cuttings of greasewood. We wrapped the arm with the leather strip, and then bound the sticks to it with strings that we cut from the sleeve. The youth came out of his faint and stared at us; then slowly sat up.

"Why have you done this? Why don't you kill me?" he signed to us with his right hand.

"We pity you! We want you to live! You are to go home with us and remain with us until your

The Dreadful River Cave

arm is strong; then you can go to your home," Dove Woman signed to him.

"Who are you?" I signed.

He tapped his breast here and there with the tips of his fingers; he was the first one of the far-away Spotted Horses People that we had ever seen.

"We are Pi-kun'-i. Come! We must go!" I signed, and gathered his bow and arrows and slipped them into the case at his back. He groaned with the pain in his arm when we helped him up on my horse. I got into the saddle, he hung onto me with his well arm, and our eager horses got us into camp quite a little time before sundown.

Our people were astonished when they saw us coming in with the young wounded man, and old Red Wing Woman made great outcry when she learned that he was an enemy. My father and Old Sun listened thoughtfully while I told them all about our discovery of the war lodges, and the medicine pouch and its contents, and what we had then done. My mother cried when I told how we had spared the young man's life, and bound his wound as well as we could.

"Oh, my man!" she said to my father, taking his hand, "now you see what this son of ours is. Brave, truly brave he is, and just as truly kind of heart: in him is the making of a great chief. I am happy! Oh, so happy!"

"Ha! One can be too kind-hearted!" said Old Sun.

I Give my Enemy His Life

My father turned to the youth and signed, "What is your name?"

"Long Bear," he answered, as well as he could with his one hand.

"Well, Long Bear," my father signed on, "we are glad that you have survived this day and are here with us. Our lodge is your lodge. Come now inside with us and we will dress your wound, and then you shall eat!"

"Yes. Of course. We must properly dress that wound," Old Sun exclaimed. "North Woman, where are you? Go quickly and bring my sack of leaf medicines. Also some new and soft leather!"

"Ha! Did n't I just hear it said that one can be too kind-hearted?" my mother laughed, making Old Sun hang his head and turn away from her, and at that we laughed with her.

I noticed now that the wounded youth was looking very sadly at me. Not so much that I had wounded him, I thought, as that I was wearing his medicine, which was no doubt as dear to him as life itself. I started off with the horses to water them, and picket them on fresh grazing-ground, and when I had done that, I took off the war clothes and returned to camp. There I put them carefully back into their parfleche case, and went into our lodge and laid it beside the youth: "Your clothing," I signed to him. "It is all there."

"You are generous. I am glad to have it back," he answered.

The Dreadful River Cave

Old Sun and my father examined his arm after my mother had washed it. They said that the bullet had not smashed the bone, but had given it a clean break and that it would soon heal. Old Sun put a layer of his medicine leaves upon the wound, and then the two of them bound it very firmly with the fresh leather, and some wide, thin splints of wood, and then laid the arm in a sling so that it would rest as easily as possible.

"There! Our work is done and I am now going to question this young Long Bear," said Old Sun.

"But see how tired he is; in what pain; and how hungry; your questions will keep!" my mother protested, as she and her helpers dished out food to us all, she herself cutting Long Bear's meat and dried backfat into convenient size for him to eat, and giving him, too, a large chunk of berry pemmican.

"I can't wait; one thing I have to know now!" the old man exclaimed, and signed to the youth: "That medicine you have, that many-colored lizard that is tied to the back of the mink, where did you get it?"

"It is not mine, nor the war clothes," he signed. "I have no medicine of my own, and was just carrying them for our chief. Back to the south, three days before we crossed Big River, we surprised an enemy war party of nine and wiped them out. Our chief took these from the man that he killed and had me carry them. Out here where we built the

I Give my Enemy His Life

war lodges, I placed the medicine case under the head of my brush couch because I thought that it might bring me a powerful dream. But I had no dream. And then I forgot all about the case until noon, when the chief asked me what I had done with it. Oh, he was angry when I told him that I had forgotten it — had left it where we slept. He sent me back for it and I was hurrying along our back trail — oh, think how surprised I was when I saw an enemy riding out at me, wearing the very clothing that I was after!"

"Well, anyhow, I know where that lizard came from," said Old Sun. "In my youth I went with a war party away south into the always-summer land and there I saw many of that kind of lizards. Oh, how beautiful they were, darting about over the sands and rocks of that strange country! I knew that they were medicine — their rainbow colors told me that — but I was young, careless, had no thought of becoming a medicine man, so took not a skin of one of them. How I wish now that I had taken one; that I had one to put in with the various skins of fur and feathers that are wrapped with my medicine pipe!"

Long Bear made no answer to that. He ceased eating, sat for some time with head down, then suddenly straightened up and signed to us: "This day I have met you, enemies, and you have proved to be friends. You could have killed me, but you have given me life and even bound up my wound. You

The Dreadful River Cave

have made your lodge my lodge, you have given me of your good food. I say to you now that, as truly as I loved my mother — she is dead — I shall never in time to come join in war against your tribe. These things that were my chief's, you gave them back to me after you had captured me although they belonged to you. I give them back to you. To you" — pointing to Old Sun — "the lizard. To you" — pointing to my father — "the war bonnet. To you"— pointing to me — "the war shirt and the medicine case."

Nothing that this stranger youth could have said or done could have pleased us more than this. Old Sun's hands really trembled as he eagerly reached over for the medicine case, opened the top cover and drew out the war bonnet and took from it the mink and the wonderful lizard bound upon its back. "How generous you are! The mink, I shall sacrifice to the gods, and pray them for your quick recovery," he signed the youth.

My father passed the war bonnet and the case with the war shirt in it to me: "My son, they are all yours; you have earned them. I am very proud of what you have done this day," he said.

I turned to Long Bear: "You shame me! I am sorry that I shot you. Out upon the plains, in the big camp of our people, I have some horses; two of them, a black of four winters, and a brown of three, shall be yours," I signed.

"Your kindness, you, and all of you, kills my

94

I Give my Enemy His Life

arm pain. I am very happy," he answered. And with that we all turned to our food and finished it.

In order to make room for our wounded guest one of my almost-mothers, Running Woman, and her two children, moved into old Red Wing Woman's lodge. We all went to sleep before the night was far gone.

Upon the following morning, when we woke up, we saw that Long Bear was having great pain in his wound; his face was very gray; his forehead at times wet with perspiration. But not once did he complain nor even groan. We all pitied him, my mother especially; she herself washed his face and hands, and cut into small portions the food that he was to eat. And after the meal was over I unbound his hair braids and combed them well, and rebraided them, wrapping their ends with some of my own mink fur strips. He was very thankful for all that we did for him.

And now Dove Woman and I had to start out again after meat, else by night there would be hungry mouths in camp. My father and Old Sun both said that by going out to the edge of the plain for buffaloes we were taking great chances of being discovered by some passing war party; they advised us to go back into the timber and hunt elk.

"What we want to do is to go to our tree hiding-place and try to kill old chief bear and his wife; but as we cannot do that to-day, but must go there be-

The Dreadful River Cave

fore they eat up the bull carcass, we shall hunt to-day where we can kill quickly plenty of meat," I told them. And we hurried out to the horses, saddled them and rode off down the ridge toward the foot of the lake.

There were many tracks of game, but none of men or of horses in the big trail that ran close to the lake. After we had crossed it, Dove Woman got down and smoothed out the tracks that our horses had left in it. We went on, crossed the river at the foot of the lake, and in the second small prairie below it saw some buffaloes. Then, as I had done on our previous meat hunt, I handed the girl my gun, got out my bow and arrows, went on ahead and ran the little herd, this time killing three of the animals, two of two years and the other a fat old cow. I had no fun in it; my thoughts were all about the thing that I wanted to do — the killing of that old chief bear. And I was cross; and so was the girl. We were cross all day as we kept going trip after trip to camp with loads of meat, and so tired when we had it all in and night had come that we could hardly sit up. We had our evening meal in my father's lodge, and Dove Woman fell asleep as soon as she finished eating her portion of the fat ribs that my mother broiled for us.

"Oh, wake up! Wake up! What do you mean by going to sleep here?" cried old Red Wing Woman, shaking the girl and pulling her up to a sitting position.

I Give my Enemy His Life

"Woman, let the girl sleep!" Old Sun told her.
"Hai! But you are the uneasy one. Always both-
ering people; always scolding; always foretelling
something bad to come! Hai! Am I not glad that
you are not my woman!"

"No more glad than I that you are not my man!
Scolder yourself!" she cried, and sprang up, seized
poor Dove Woman by the arm, and dragged her
to the doorway and out of the lodge.

My father quietly smiled: "Old Sun, my friend,
she had the last word," he said. And at that we all
laughed. We looked at the old man and laughed
again; from the appearance of his face we knew
that he was all on fire with anger.

My father turned to our wounded one and signed:
"We haven't questioned you because you have been
in so much pain. But now, if you feel like it, you
can tell us about your people, where they are
camped, and whither is going the war party that
you were with."

It was not easy for the youth to do that with the
use of but one hand, but we made out from his
signs that, when he left his people, they were encamped in some mountains to the south and east
of the mouth of Elk River,[1] and that the party he
had been with was hoping to find a camp of the
Blackfeet and run off a big band of their horses.
Failing in that, they intended to cross our mountains and raid the herds of the Blue Paint People;

[1] The Yellowstone River.

The Dreadful River Cave

or of any other tribe living upon the plains of the Other-Side Big River.[1]

"Then they will cross the mountains," my father told him, "because they will find no Blackfeet north of here along the foot of the mountains: they are all well out upon the plains, and will remain there until late in the summer."

We thought it very strange that his war party had seen nothing of our own great camp moving up to Point-of-Rocks River, but made no mention of that to him.

I was not at all sleepy; my mind was so full of what I hoped to do on the next day that I felt I could not sleep. I turned to Long Bear and began signing to him all about the old chief bear and his wife and children, and he became so interested that, for the time, I believe he forgot the pain in his arm. When I had done he signed that he would like above all things to go with me after the bear if he were only well enough, and added that he would pray to his gods to give me success.

"Yes. And we must pray our gods for that, too," said my father, and filled and passed a pipe to Old Sun. By turns they both smoked and prayed to the gods for Dove Woman and me to come home with the claws of the sticky mouths, and with whole bodies. And then the three of us sang over and over the song of the wolf, ever the good-luck song of the hunter. But we sang it very low so that

---

[1] The Columbia River.

I Give my Enemy His Life

no sound of it might go echoing down into the valley or up the ridge to the ears of any possibly nearby enemy. And having done that, Old Sun went home and we all lay down and fell asleep.

Came the great day — or at least I hoped it was — a day of cloudless sky and windless too.

While we were eating our morning meal I heard Dove Woman call out to me from her lodge: "Almost-brother, have you finished eating?"

"Not yet," I answered.

"Well, hurry, let us go down to our watching-place!" she cried.

"No, not until the middle of the day. Not until the hot sun drives the bears deep into the cool swamp," I replied.

And then, after a time, we heard old Red Wing Woman scolding her: "No, you are not going out to water those horses!" she commanded. "Your almost-brother can do that. You, lazy one, shall sit right here and help me cut all of this meat into shape for drying."

And then Old Sun roared out from his lodge: "No! No! Woman, those who are to go against sticky mouths may not use knife nor awl nor needle lest they cut themselves or pierce their flesh; should they do that, then the chances are that they will be clawed by the sticky mouths!"

"Medicine man," she shrieked, "will you never cease interfering in my affairs? I do not want your advice nor your orders. I pass on to you the words

The Dreadful River Cave

that Bear Eagle recently gave to me: Man, 'absolutely close your mouth'!"

Unseemly though it was for a woman thus to address a man, and a great medicine man at that, we could not help laughing, all but my mother, who said: "The quarreling of those two distresses me. It may lead up to something worse than angry words. Old though she is, I am going this day to give Red Wing Woman some advice. If I can bring it about, there shall be nothing but kind thoughts and gentle speech in this our little camp."

She went at once over to the old woman's lodge, and when I, a little later, started to care for the horses I found Dove Woman watering them. She laughed as she said to me: "Well, almost-brother, you see that I am released from the meat-cutting. But, oh, is n't grandmother angry this morning!"

I was eager as the girl to start for our watching-place. I watched the sun trail up and up into the blue and never had it seemed to go so slowly. We sat a long time with my father and Old Sun and the wounded one out in the shade of the trees, half-listening to their talk, ourselves having nothing to say. The women worked hard outside the lodges, and the bushes roundabout soon became red with the sheets of meat they hung upon them to dry. The children had been forbidden to shout or to make any outcry in their play, but this morning they became very noisy, and Old Sun ordered them

I Give my Enemy His Life

brought before us for a good scolding, which they got and were then made to sit in a row in front of us.

Well, at last the time came for us to go. We went for our weapons, I taking my bow as well as my gun, and off we hurried down the hill. But we slowed up as we approached our watching-place and saw many freshly broken trails of meat-eaters through the grass and the thick growths of pea-vines, all the trails running toward our kill; we feared that it had all been devoured. But presently we heard meat birds quarreling off under the three cottonwoods, and by that we knew that some of the carcass remained, and that right then there were no bears nor other animals at it. We pushed on through the brush, and like a small cloud were the birds that flew up when they saw us. We ran to our tree and I climbed up into it, and then Dove Woman passed up the guns and was soon beside me upon our brush-laid, comfortable scaffold. We looked down upon the carcass of the bull: there was still some meat upon its legs and back, and the head had not been touched. We were glad, for we now felt sure that we were this day to see old chief bear and his wife come to feed upon it.

Never were there such greedy ones as the birds that we had frightened away from the carcass. They came back upon it as soon as they saw us sit quiet upon our watching-place, and some, so full of meat that they could hold no more, just stood upon the best places and kept driving off those that

The Dreadful River Cave

were really hungry. And came now the wisest meat-eater of all the winged kind, a raven, first circling around and around above us and loudly, hoarsely croaking, and then diving down through the trees and settling upon the carcass, all the other birds fluttering up into the branches — some right over our heads — and scolding at him. We were glad that he came, that bird of good luck, medicine bird that he was. He was not long in tearing out with his strong beak all the meat that he wanted, and as he flew away I called out to him to return and feast upon our meat as often as he would.

Why is the raven great medicine? you ask. Because it is a sun bird. You will remember that when our great ancestor, Scar Face, visited the sun, he was given a raven's tail feather to take back to earth as the sign that he was the bearer of the sky god's messages to the people.

Well, the meat birds again fluttered down upon the carcass, but were soon driven away by a band of seven wolves that came to feast upon it. There was now a little breeze from the west; they had come from the east, passing right under our watching-place, but they never smelled us, never once looked up toward us. But now and then one of them would cease feeding and move off a little way toward the swamp, or to the west or north of the carcass, and sniff the air and set his head sideways and look and listen for the enemy. There was the odor of bear all about the place — we ourselves could

I Give my Enemy His Life

sometimes smell it — and there was no doubt but what some of the wolves had been followers of the old chief wolf that the chief bear's wife had killed. She was the enemy they were expecting would come and they were taking no chances with her.

We were keeping little watch to the east of us; no more than the wolves were we expecting the bears to come from that direction, but happening to look off that way I saw a bush quiver, and then caught a glimpse of a bear passing it and heading our way. I nudged Dove Woman, sitting close to me on my left, and slightly motioned with my head the way she was to look. We had already learned that, well up from the ground as we were, we could make some little movement without being discovered by the wolves. Right there and then I learned something that I had never thought of: the meat-eaters never look for prey or enemy, nor the grass-eaters for their many enemies, at a level higher than themselves. Bear that in mind when you go out to watch for game.

Haï! How excited I became when I again saw the bear, or rather just the dim shape of him passing through some brush still nearer us. I noiselessly cocked my gun and Dove Woman, watching me, did the same with her gun. She, too, had made out that it was a bear approaching us and was even more excited than I; she was slightly trembling. I leaned over and hissed into her ear: "Be firm! Calm yourself!"

CHAPTER VII

DOVE WOMAN AND I MAKE A BIG KILLING

NEARER and nearer the bear came, working his way through thick brush and making it bend and quiver, and at last stepped out into a little opening, and to our great surprise we saw that it was neither the old chief bear, nor his wife, but just a common black bear. I could hardly believe that he was real! How my eyes had deceived me! How terribly disappointed I was! I heard my almost sister whisper: "Kyai-yo! A nothing bear!"

We saw at once that this bear had never been at the carcass; the gentle west wind was carrying to him the odor of meat and he was following it up. But how cautiously, more and more slowly as his nose told him that he was near the source of the odor. He came on with the noiseless, sneaking, carefully placed tread of a lynx when approaching a rabbit; and every little way he sat up and looked off ahead. He came to the last patch of willows between him and the carcass, sneaked around it, and sat up, and the wolves instantly saw him and in their surprise sprang away from the carcass before they clearly saw just what he was — nothing but a black bear. Back they came to the carcass. Two

We Make a Big Killing

or three times he loudly snorted at them; they would not take fright at that; he got down upon all four feet and sidled off to the north of the carcass and the wolves, and sat down to wait until they should go away and leave him to take his share of the feast.

Just then it was that we heard a dry stick snap somewhere off in the direction of the swamp. The wolves heard it, too, ceased eating and stood with heads well up and listening, and as quickly as I can spat my hands they were gone from there, off whence they came with all the haste that they could make. For they had seen what we saw before they did, the approach of the old wife bear and her young. And now, not far behind her, came the old chief bear, still upon three feet and holding the burned, sore foot well up from the ground. On they came without pause, looking neither to right nor left, intent only upon the feast awaiting them. The black bear, his enemies gone, was also approaching the carcass. He got to it first, stuck his head well down under the back and tore off a large strip of meat, drew back to chew and swallow it, and saw the old wife almost upon him. If the wolves had been quick to flee from her he was quicker, just a streak of bounding black fur vanishing into the brush. The old wife gave just one loud snort and moved on to the carcass and began tearing meat from a hind leg, her young leaving her heels and moving off beyond the carcass.

The Dreadful River Cave

And now came the old chief bear, shouldering her out of the place she had chosen and ripping out a big piece of meat with his powerful jaws. Almost I gasped out loud when I saw how very large he was; not so long-legged as a buffalo, of course, but fully as heavy and long-bodied as an old bull. He stood full side to me; I could aim at either of the sure-death places I chose, just back of the shoulder and low down to pierce the heart, or at a point just below the ear to strike the brain. I aimed for the heart; even if I missed it I would give him a death-shot through his lungs. I silently called upon the gods to give me steady hands and clear eyes. I took long aim and pulled the trigger.

Oh, what a terrible roar of pain and anger that old chief bear let out when my gun boomed and the bullet spatted into him! Through the powder-smoke I saw him give his old wife a fierce blow upon her shoulder with his uninjured paw that almost knocked her down. She roared and staggered out of his way, and he turned and bit at his wound, roaring again and again. The smoke lifted and I saw that blood was gushing from his nose and mouth, that I had no need to shoot him again. He turned again toward his wife, and she seemed suddenly to know — perhaps the life-blood streaming from him told her — that a terrible enemy of her kind was somewhere thereabout. But where? She backed away from him, her young now closely hugging her sides, and turned, looking this way and

We Make a Big Killing

that way and came straight toward us. I reached out for Dove Woman's gun. She pushed away my hand: "No! I shall kill her!" she whispered, and leaned out over the platform to take aim.

"No! You will miss! Give me that gun!" I insisted. But she had no ears for what I whispered, nor did I dare take the gun from her. And just then the old wife turned about and sat up, back toward us, looking, looking, sniffing, sniffing for she knew not what, and at last staring straight at her old man, staggering toward her as though for help and hoarsely gasping for breath. And then, after long aim, Dove Woman fired at the old wife. Boom! A dark cloud of powder-smoke drifted up into my face; it cleared away and I saw the old wife lying flat and motionless upon her side. Twice, three times she opened and shut her quivering forepaws, gritting her teeth, and then with a last shuddering of her whole body her jaws dropped open and she was dead. In front of her, not two steps off, her old man was making a last effort to keep upon his feet; he slowly sank to the ground and rested his head upon his forepaws and breathed his last; it was as though he had stretched out there for a rest and had gone to sleep. There remained the three young ones. When Dove Woman fired and their mother fell, they ran squalling about here and there in the brush and then came back to her body. I began shooting them with my bow and arrows. Seven arrows I fired and then they, too, were dead. Dove

The Dreadful River Cave

Woman was the first to speak; she spoke like one half-asleep: "We have wiped them out!" she said.

"Yes, they are dead; their shadows are on the way to the Sandhills," I answered.

I reloaded her gun, then mine. She slid to the ground and I passed down to her the weapons and got down myself. We examined first her kill, then mine. We had little to say to one another; what we had done was too big to talk about just at first. We had to get used to it. Upon the left shoulder of the old chief bear was a hairless, healed-over scar. I felt something hard there under the skin, cut into it, and drew out an arrowhead: "Almost-sister," I said, "I believe that I have killed the killer of Flying Elk!"

"What a *coup* for you! And I killed the killer's wife!" she cried. "See, here is where I aimed. Come, feel what the bullet did." I felt the place; the bullet had smashed into the back of the bear's skull; it was no wonder that she had dropped so suddenly!

"Let us cut off these claws and go home as quickly as we can," she proposed.

"Our people will be wanting to see these great bears; we will bring them here and then cut off the claws," I told her, and away we went for camp.

Our people had heard the *boom! boom!* of our guns and were all gathered out in front of my father's lodge anxiously watching for our return. As soon as they saw us the women and children came running to meet us: "You have killed the old

We Make a Big Killing

bears! I can tell by your faces that you have killed them!" my mother cried.

"We have wiped them out!" I signed, and passed on to tell my father and Old Sun all about it, while Dove Woman told the others, and as I talked I made the signs for what I said, so that Long Bear could know what we had done. They all, men and women, seemed to be more excited over our success than we were, Old Sun especially.

"Now is it proven that our medicines are again powerful!" he cried out to my father. "The gods have accepted our smoke offerings; they have listened to our prayers for the safety and success of these our children. Come! Let us go down to the kills and sacrifice them to the sun!"

Long Bear insisted upon going with us and I saddled a horse for him, for he was so weak from loss of blood that he could not walk far. Old Sun got his pipe and smoking-things together, and got upon the other horse with my father. Dove Woman and I led the way, the people all scattered out behind us so as to leave no noticeable trail, and we soon brought them to our kills. How they stared at them, exclaiming again and again at the great size of the old chief bear and his wife, and staring up at our platform in the tree, asking more questions than we could answer — that is, the women and children and Long Bear did. My father and Old Sun stood off to one side talking together, saying nothing to us, but came close up when Dove Woman

The Dreadful River Cave

began cutting off the foreclaws of her kill and I the foreclaws of mine. Said my father then, when we had severed the last ones:

"Be quiet now, all of you. As these animals are themselves great medicine, we medicine men are forbidden to kill them, or to use their hides for robes, or even to mention them by their right name. But we are permitted to take strips of their fur to fasten to the stems of our sacred pipes. We shall, therefore, take each of us a strip from the back of this old chief sticky mouth, killer, we believe, of our friend Flying Elk. We proceed to cut the strips."

They did so, my father first, each cutting out a strip the width of a finger, and about three hands in length. Old Sun then filled his pipe, my father lighted it, and, after blowing smoke to the four world directions, cried out to the sun that we sacrificed to him the bodies of the old chief sticky mouth and his wife and children. "And therefore," he concluded, "we pray you to look with favor upon our medicines. Guard us from all dangers that we may grow and gather a great harvest to the sacred nah-wak'-o-sis that we have planted. Give us all, we pray you, long life and happiness."

"Yes! Yes! Pity us! Pity us all!" we cried. And with a last look at the bodies of old chief bear and his wife, went homeward up the ridge in the fading light of this great day.

"Now, now, almost-sister," I said to Dove

We Make a Big Killing

Woman, "we are free! There is plenty of meat in camp; to-morrow we can again go to the falls and watch for that Under-Water person!"

We were a very happy camp of people that night, the women especially, for there was no longer in their hearts the constant dread of the old chief bear, of what he might at any time do to their little ones and to them. True, there were other real bears — oh, plenty of them — but it was thought that they were harmless, quick enough to run from sight or odor of man.

After we had finished our evening meal Long Bear asked me to explain to him what my father had prayed for down there in the valley by the bear carcasses, and so for the first time he learned why we were separated from the great camp of our people; that we were hiding there in the timber for the purpose of growing nah-wak'-o-sis, and this at the risk of our lives. He signed that he thought we were very brave.

"Not very brave," my father signed to him, "but strong in the faith that our medicine will keep us safe in our great undertaking — that is, so long as we ourselves use good sense and caution in all that we do. The gods do not love foolish people. Some time back we were foolish; we made them smoke offerings of rank, white men's tobacco and offended them; we failed in all that we undertook. We threw that tobacco away and resumed the use of our own sacred smoking-leaves, and lo! our med-

The Dreadful River Cave

icine became again powerful. So, you see, it is very important that we raise a great quantity of the sacred leaves, not only for ourselves, but for the other medicine men of our tribe."

"My people never use the white men's smoking-leaves, and only the kind that we have always raised when smoking to the gods," Long Bear signed. "We laugh at the men of the Earth Lodges tribes,[1] whom we often visit; they are never without pipes in their mouths — smoking, smoking all the time, and therefore become so lazy that they will not go out of sight of their camps to hunt. They depend upon us for dry meat and leather and tanned robes, trading us dried corn for them."

And so we talked on and on far into the night about many things, and then went happily to sleep.

I awoke with the coming of the first faint white light of the new day, aroused my mother and asked her to get up and prepare food for us; went over and thumped the lodge of Red Wing Woman until she awoke and scolded me, and Dove Woman answered my call; and I watered and re-picketed the horses. I bathed, returned to our lodge, and dressed Long Bear's hair — as I did every morning — and then dressed my own and painted myself. Dove Woman came in, washed and painted, her long hair freshly braided, and we had our early meal. I told my father that we were going to the falls to

[1] The Mandans and Minnetavees.

We Make a Big Killing

watch for the Under-Water person. He said that we had much better go away up the valley on discovery, and I answered that we should do both. We took up our weapons and left camp before the sun began to redden the mountain-tops.

The falls were still in deep shadow when we arrived at our watching-place behind the juniper brush and looked down at them. We noticed that there was much more water pouring over the top of the cliff than when we had last been there; the hot sun was now melting the deep snow upon the high mountain-tops. Otters were fishing in the deep pool, as usual, and hurrying off downstream with their catches. Great clouds of spray from the upper fall now almost hid the dark mouth of the river cave from view; the little strip of sand upon which we had seen the tracks of the Under-Water person was now itself under water. We remained there behind the brush until the sun was almost halfway up to the middle of the blue. Under-Water People might be in the dark cave, probably were there, but, as Dove Woman said, most likely asleep. I told her that we should go up the valley for a look around and return for a late afternoon watch upon the river cave.

From our hiding-place we climbed to the top of the cañon, and then went quartering up westward along the side of a very high, red-rock mountain, then unnamed, but which we now call Rising Wolf Mountain, after that wholly good and generous

The Dreadful River Cave

white man who has been so long a member of our tribe.[1] The mountain is sparsely timbered and has many clifflike outcroppings along its side, and for that reason it is a favorite feeding-ground of bighorns and white goats. From the time we began its ascent we followed one trail after another of these animals, and after a while saw numbers of both kinds of them resting, and some feeding, well up above the edge of the timber from which rises the very steep and bare summit of the mountain. We then ceased climbing and kept a level course on westward, for we did not want to alarm the animals; to do that would be a sure way for us to attract the attention of any of our enemies who might be in the valley.

It was about the middle of the day when we sneaked out upon a brushy ledge of the mountain-side from which we could see every part of the great valley, and there we sat down for a long rest. Directly below us lay the upper lake of the Two Medicine, a small prairie at the foot of it, and at its head rose a very steep, narrow mountain of black rock of such peculiar shape that our fathers in the long ago had named it Rising Bull Mountain. This great rise of rock, timbered only upon its lower slopes, separated the valley into two forks, the left one, heavily timbered, running far back to the snow- and ice-capped summit of the range,

[1] Hugh Monroe. He became a member of the Pi-kun-i in 1816.

114

We Make a Big Killing

the right fork, in which there was a small, narrow pond, ending near by in a basin walled with very high cliffs. Opposite us a long, thickly timbered, brush-edged point ran out into the lake. At the end of the point was a strip of sandy shore, and there we saw a band of elk come out to drink and splash about in the water; they were the only living things in sight in all the valley so far as we could determine. There was not a least flurry of wind to disturb the surface of the lake; the mountains and the point were shadowed upside down upon it. No leaping trout broke its calm with widening circles; it was a fishless lake; that fallen mountain lying across the valley below, with its falls and somewhere-choked-full river cave, prevented them swimming up into it. Dove Woman said that Old Man, when he saw what his carelessness had done, should have made at least a few trout to grow and increase in the lake. I told her that the great World-Maker had had no time to put fish into every last one of his lakes and ponds; that he had doubtless put them into his big rivers and told them to scatter out as they could into the smaller streams and the lakes.

After watching the valley for a long time and becoming quite certain that there was no camp of the enemy in it, we descended to the shore of the lake and followed down its outlet, finding much fresh beaver sign along its brush-grown banks, and more than once seeing deer and elk running off into

The Dreadful River Cave

the heavy timber upon our near approach to them. For some distance down from the lake the outlet flowed smoothly between firm banks, then brokenly over a bed of rough stones, until, at last, the greater part of the water went swirling and gurgling down under a pile of large boulders choking the head of the river cave. We carefully examined this place, but could find not one of the disappearing stream-lets that was large enough to suck down a man, nor anything larger than a half-grown beaver. Here was no passageway for the Under-Water People. We wondered if they, like other water creatures, otters, beavers, and mink, made trips overland from stream to stream and lake to lake.

The amount of water that flowed on past the bed of boulders made but a small stream, so small that we could in places jump across it. Quite often on our way along it we would stop and listen for the sound of the larger stream that we knew was below us, rushing on and on through the dark cave to its fall at the face of the cliff, quite a long way ahead, but not once did we even faintly hear it.

We had followed the stream about halfway from the boulders to the edge of the cliff when we came upon something that startled us: in a strip of sand along the shore were the barefooted tracks of a per-son who had been traveling up the course of the stream! They were not old, no more than a day or two, and were about the size of my own footprints, by no means large.

We Make a Big Killing

Said Dove Woman: "Whoever made these tracks made also those that we found in the sandy little point at the pool."

"That is also my belief," I told her.

We were very uneasy; we looked back up the stream whence we had come, and down the stream, and stared into the timber; we could see nothing suspicious, but well knew that the maker of the tracks might be watching us from some near-by point. We were afraid to stand there any longer. We were upon the south side of the stream. "Let us cross over and get into the timber as soon as we can," I told the girl.

I led on down the shore to a narrowing of the stream, where we jumped across it, and there we again came upon the person's tracks in some sand, and upon this shore he had been walking down toward the cliff. It was impossible for us to determine which way he had first gone. If downstream, then he had gone back toward the summit of the range; if upstream first, then he was now somewhere below us.

"Almost-brother," the girl whispered to me, "as surely as we stand here, these tracks were made by an Under-Water person, by the one who I so plainly saw going into the darkness of the river cave. I believe that he is down there in the cave right now!"

"You may be right. We will go to our hiding-place and watch for him," I said, and away we went

The Dreadful River Cave

up into the timber and along the mountain-side, then down over the rim of the cañon and along it to the juniper brush.

The pool and the falls were now in deep shadow, for the day was far gone, the sun about to go down behind the great range. Not a living thing was in sight, not even a shore bird. The falls seemed to roar louder than we had ever heard them and more hoarsely. I somehow felt that water itself had a language and was trying to make me understand it. I thought that it was trying to tell me about the terrible creatures that were living there in the river cave, and warning me to go away from the place and never return to it.

"Roar-talk as you will, oh, water, you shall not make an afraid heart of me," I told it. "Before I leave this Two Medicine country I am going to know all about that black hole from which you are pouring and foaming!"

"What is that you are saying?" Dove Woman asked.

"Nothing much; just talking to that roaring falls," I answered.

"Ha! It makes me feel sad. It makes me shiver," she said.

Just then I caught the movement of something in the brush across the cañon and high above the pool. I thought surely that we were about to see the one for whom we had so long been looking. "Get ready to shoot. There, across from us, I saw

We Make a Big Killing

the brush move!" I told the girl, and cocked my gun and half-raised it.

Again we were disappointed, for instead of the person we expected to see it was a big mountain lion that came out from the brush and stood upon a bare rock, staring down at the rocks and brush below and gently swaying and twitching his long tail. He suddenly went leaping down from rock to rock almost to the edge of the pool, then whirled about and felt in between two brush-covered logs and brought out a squalling rabbit fast in the clutch of his right paw. Perhaps he was not hungry; anyhow, he intended to have some fun with the rabbit before killing it, for he released it, allowed it to run off a little way, then leaped and caught it again. Three times he did this, and the fourth time the rabbit all but got away from him; he caught it just as it was half into a hole under a rock and gave it a toss that sent it end over end away up into the air, such a sudden and far-flung toss that he failed to see what way it went. He stood motionless, tail toward the pool, listening for it to come down. But the rabbit never struck the ground; it fell right into the falls and was carried down into the foaming depths of the pool; and almost at once came to the surface, and swam rapidly to our side of the swirling water, and disappeared among the rocks and brush that bordered the shore.

Almost we laughed aloud at the surprise of that old seizer when he failed to hear the thud of the

The Dreadful River Cave

rabbit upon the near-by rocks. He sprang suddenly
around and stared up into the air, whirled about
and looked up again; and then he began circling
among the rocks, sniffing at the dark places under
them, pawing the brush between them, and after
a long search seeming to realize that he had lost his
prey. Anyhow, with a last long look around he gave
up all hope of finding it and went sneaking off down
along the shore of the stream and passed out of our
sight. It had been hard for me to resist the temptation to shoot him, for I had long wanted the skin
of a seizer for a saddle robe. Only once or twice in
a lifetime did a hunter get a chance to kill one of
the timid animals; this was my second opportunity
to shoot one. If, now, we failed to count *coup* upon
the Under-Water person, I knew that I should always regret letting this opportunity pass.

"Almost-brother, the sun is about to enter his
lodge; it is time for us to go home," Dove Woman
told me.

"But his wife will soon appear and give us plenty
of light. We will remain here for a time," I decided.

CHAPTER VIII

MORE DISCOVERIES

BETWEEN the going-down of the sun and the appearance of Night-Light, not long afterward, the night was very dark; and even when she arose above the eastern rim of the great valley, shining right into our eyes, we could not see the pool, and the falls were but a dim, whitish blur in the blackness of the deep cañon. I had not taken thought of what the conditions would be and was ashamed of my lack of foresight. A whole tribe of Under-Water People might be moving about down there and we should be unable to see them. And supposing it was true — as I suspected it was — that they went about upon the land as easily as they swam in the water? Why, they could surround us, capture us, do with us as they would. Apparently my almost-sister was thinking the same thing, for she leaned over and whispered to me: "Black Elk, I am afraid. That blackness down there may be hiding terrible things from us. Come, let us go home!"

It was mean of me to put all the blame of our going upon her, but I did. "We must remain. Night-Light will be shining down into the cañon toward the middle of the night and enable us to see plainly the pool and the falls, and any one moving about there," I told her.

The Dreadful River Cave

"No, no! I am shaking with fear! Right now those terrible Under-Water People may be coming to seize us. Almost-brother, as you love your mother, I beg you to take me away from here," she pleaded. "Oh, well, if that is the way you feel I must do as you say," I agreed.

And just then from down there in the black darkness of the cañon, along with the roar of the falls there came to us the sound of a voice as if in earnest prayer to the gods. There was no mistaking it, although we could not catch the words. Dove Woman sprang to her feet, seized my arm and pulled me up beside her, and hand in hand we backed away from the juniper brush until sure that we could not be seen from below, then turned and fled for camp. There was plenty of light in the timber for us to see our way. I let the girl take the lead and closely followed her, looking back quite often to see if we were pursued.

We were all but out of breath when we sighted camp. There was a fire only in my father's lodge, so we knew that the people were all assembled there and anxiously awaiting our return. Dove Woman thrust aside the door curtain and burst in upon them, I right after her, and they instantly saw by our faces that fear was in our hearts. The women shrank far from us, old Red Wing Woman crying out: "Oh, what is it? What has happened to you?" and all the younger children shrieking and taking shelter in their mothers' arms.

More Discoveries

"Hai! Hai! Be quiet, crazy women! You children cease crying at once!" Old Sun hissed so fiercely that the noise instantly ceased.

My father motioned me to a seat beside him, but asked no question. He did not need to, for Dove Woman broke out: "Oh, medicine men! Oh, my grandmother! You will hardly believe what we have seen and heard: tracks of an Under-Water person in the sand along the stream above the falls! And just now, away down in the black darkness at the foot of the falls, even above its roar we heard an Under-Water person!"

She stopped for want of breath. My father looked at me then, questioningly, and I told just where we had been and all that we had seen and heard since leaving camp that morning. None interrupted me. I finished my tale, and still no one spoke. So I said: "Father, and you, Old Sun, you two are very wise. I want you to tell me what you think about this: Was it really an Under-Water person who made the tracks we saw, whose voice we heard, or were they the tracks and the voice of a real person — a man of one of the enemy tribes?"

"Ha! Bear Eagle, my friend, that is a question we cannot at once answer!" Old Sun exclaimed. "Let us go back; let us think of all that has been handed down to us about the Under-Water People. Now, as to the tracks that these young ones have twice seen in the sand, below the falls and above them. So far as I can remember, none of the tales

The Dreadful River Cave

about the Under-Water People even once mention their ever having been seen upon the land — "

"True enough," my father interrupted, "but you will recall that our long-ago ancestor who visited them in their lodges, deep down upon the bottom of Old Man's River, was feasted by them and strawberries were a part of the feast. It follows that they do leave the water and walk about upon the land, else they could not have had strawberries."

"Right you are! Proof enough that they do go about upon the land," Old Sun agreed. "And of course they have voices: they talked with that deep-diving ancestor of ours."

"Remember, too, that some days back we saw a person going up into the river cave," Dove Woman put in.

"True. And I cannot believe that a real person, a man of our tribes or our enemy tribes, would dare attempt to go up into that black hole. My opinion is that it is an Under-Water person who is living down there in the cave and wandering up and down the stream," said Old Sun.

"My friend, we have no proof of it," my father told him. "He who walked along the sands, who cried out down there in the dark cañon, who the children saw going up behind the falls, may be an Under-Water person, and he may be a real person. My friend, I feel very uneasy about this. But we have our medicines. I advise you to pray hard this night for a revealing dream. I will do so, too, and

thus, perhaps, we may solve this mystery of the
cañon."

"Right you are! I shall pray hard for a vision!"
the old man exclaimed.

"If he is an Under-Water person," said my
father, more to himself than to us, "we need have
little fear of him; none of his kind were ever known
to come into one of our camps. But if he is a real
person there is no end to the harm that he may do
us if he learns that we are camping here."

"Na-ye-ya'! This is terrible! You medicine men,
this is great trouble you have got my poor grandchild and me into by bringing us up here!" old
Red Wing Woman wailed.

"Now, is n't that just what you could expect of
her!" Old Sun snorted. "Followed us up, insisted
upon coming with us, and then puts all the blame
on us when trouble arises!"

"Woman, come you with me and my women,"
he added. "I need your voice in the medicine songs
that we shall sing." And strange to say, she followed them out of our lodge without one protest.

My father and mother began painting themselves preparatory to taking down his medicine
pipe, and while they were doing that I explained to
Long Bear in the sign language what all our talk
had been about. He was greatly interested, and
when I had done he signed me that he was very
poor feeling because he was unable to go with Dove
Woman and me upon our hunts and our trails of

The Dreadful River Cave

discovery here and there. In his opinion the man in the cañon was no Under-Water person: he was a passing wanderer from one of our enemy tribes.

Never had I heard my father make such heart-lifting prayers as he did that night after we had all joined in singing the unwrapping songs, and his sacred water-medicine pipestem lay exposed to view. His voice trembled as he besought the gods to give us all long, full life; to make our sacred planting grow to full and heavy leaf; to give him that very night a revealing vision of the person in the cañon. And, finally, he called Dove Woman and me to sit before him, and painted us with the sacred red, praying that we, the eyes, the ears, the defenders of our little camp, be given the power to outwit and wipe out the man in the cañon, no matter what he proved to be, an Under-Water person or just a common enemy.

His prayers did me good, let me tell you; they made me ashamed of my cowardice in running away from the cañon and putting the blame of our going upon my almost-sister. They gave me courage to continue my quest of the enemy, even, if necessary, to go into that black hole in the cliff and there attack him. So, anyhow, I felt at that time. Yes, I said to myself that, if I could get the Under-Water person in no other way, I should go into the river cave after him were it possible for me to ascend the falls.

Well, our medicine prayers and songs came to an

More Discoveries

end and my mother put carefully away the medicine, and then set before Dove Woman and me the food that we so much needed. From Old Sun's lodge there came to us the faint singing of his thunder-pipe songs.

It died away, and Red Wing Woman returned: "This night I am afraid. My girl and I shall sleep here," she said.

"You may have my couch. Long Bear and I will go to your lodge," I told her.

We went there as soon as I finished eating. Night-Light was shining straight down through the smoke-hole, enabling us to see the two couches and everything else that was there. I put extra robes upon one of the couches for Long Bear and made him comfortable, and lay down upon the other. We soon slept.

An ear-piercing burst of thunder awakened us, the first thunder of the summer. Heavy rain was beating down upon the lodge skin. Came more thunder right over our little camp, and with it flash after flash of lightning that made the night like day. Never had I heard such loud thunder nor seen such continuous, blinding lightning. I cried out to Thunder Bird to have pity upon us all and turn his arrows of dreadful fire away from our lodges. He did take pity on us; he flew on up over the rocky peaks of the mountains, and there for a long time roared and shot his terrible fire until, at last, somewhere to the south, old Wind-Maker got angry at him

The Dreadful River Cave

and fanned up with his big ears a terrible wind that drove him off to the north. He was somewhere above the head of Cutbank River when we heard the last of him. It was well for us that we were camped in the shelter of the timber, else our lodges would have been blown down by the wind. It did blow down several trees that stood near us. It did not last long; it chased on after Thunder Bird, driving him clear out of the country, and then the rain settled down to a heavy and steady fall. Day was breaking. I got up and dressed, helped Long Bear to put on his clothing, and we hurried over to my father's lodge, where a fire was already burning.

Old Sun came into the lodge right after us. "Well, my friend, although my prayers brought me no vision, they did bring the rain for which I also asked," he said to my father as soon as he was seated. "We badly needed it; the earth of our sacred planting-place was becoming very dry. But how was it with you — had you a vision?"

"A part of one," my father answered. "I did not fall asleep until long after the fire died out, long after the middle of the night. Then almost at once, so it seemed, my shadow went forth upon discovery. As I remember it I went from here straight down to the river, and followed it up looking for tracks in every strip of mud and sand. Plenty of tracks there were of elk and deer and bears and wolves, and smaller creatures, but none of man. Ahead, after a time, I heard the roar of the falls. I

More Discoveries

went on and on up the narrowing cañon, came to the last bend in it, and cautiously leaned out and looked up toward the falls, and there, just below them and at the left side of the deep pool, I saw a splash in the water as if a large body had suddenly dived into it. No otter nor beaver nor bird could have made such a big splash. 'Ha! That must have been an Under-Water person! Now, when he comes up I shall take careful aim and kill him!' I said. I cocked my gun and raised it, stood watching the surface of the pool — and then, suddenly, no more vision: thunder had broken it and I was wide awake here upon my couch."

"Ha! How unfortunate! And just as the mystery was about to be revealed to you!" Old Sun exclaimed.

"I say that it is revealed! It is plain enough to me!" Red Wing Woman cried. "As the splash was too big for any water animal to have made, no other than an Under-Water person made it!"

"There, chiefs! There is truth for you!" my mother said, and all the women agreed with her.

But my father gave her no answer, nor did Old Sun. I myself, having seen otters fishing in the pool and well knowing how much commotion they could make, believed that it was the splash of one of them that my father had seen in his vision. I did not tell my thought.

"Well, my friend and people all, if the rain ceases and the sun comes out, this is my great day," Old

The Dreadful River Cave

Sun said to us. "From far to the south Thunder Bird has again returned to us, bringing his rains to water our plains and mountains so that all things that grow upon them may have full life. Therefore, upon this first day of his return I have to unwrap my thunder pipe and smoke and pray to him. I ask you all to help me."

"That we will do, and gladly. And while we are about it let us make the ceremony as complete as we possibly can do it," my father answered.

"All through the long winter — safe hidden from the sharp eyes and searching hands of the children — I have kept a small sack of dried, last summer's berries for this great ceremony; they are yours if you need them," my mother told the old medicine man.

"Sings Alone Woman, never in all our tribe was there so thoughtful, careful, and provident a wife as you," Old Sun all but shouted to her. "Would that my women were like you! Berries we had in plenty, but they have too often made us feasts of them and given them to this one and that one, to all who asked. Gladly I accept your offering, for of our drying there are only a few handfuls left."

"Old Sun, you must cease praising this woman of mine, else she will become so proud of herself that it will be impossible for us to live in the same lodge with her," my father scolded. But we knew that he did not mean what he said. Ah, yes. The great love and honor that he had for my mother,

More Discoveries

and his other wives too, was as boundless as the sky above us. It is the most pleasant of all the pleasant memories of my youth.

Well, we had our early morning meal, Old Sun eating with us. The rain continued to fall; every depression in the ground around our camp became a small pond of water. We talked of many things as the morning passed, but mostly about the mysterious person in the cañon and about my father's vision. We could be sure of nothing, but Old Sun, my father, my mother, Red Wing Woman, and all the other women believed that the strange one actually was an Under-Water person. So did Dove Woman, who said again and again: "There can be no doubt about it: he is an Under-Water person; with my own eyes I saw him!"

I listened to them all, but said nothing. More and more I had the feeling that I must go into the river cave and see what was there.

After a time I asked Dove Woman to go with me to care for the horses, and when we were well away from the camp I said to her: "I am ashamed of myself. Last night I let you beg me to lead you away from the cañon — from the sound of that strange voice down in its blackness. I want to tell you that I was just as scared as you were; that even before you spoke I wanted to run for home."

"Almost-brother, I am glad you tell me that. I have been fearing that you were angry with me for begging you to run from the cañon. So we were

The Dreadful River Cave

both afraid! Let us never watch there again at night," she said.

"Never again at night," I promised.

The horses would not drink. We picketed them upon fresh grass and vines and returned to the lodge. Soon afterward the rain ceased falling and the sun broke through the clouds. They lifted from the mountains and drifted off to the east. Old Sun had hurried home with his present of dried service-berries. He soon called out to us that he was about to take down his sacred pipe, and we all gathered in his lodge.

The old man and his head wife, North Woman, had already painted themselves with the sacred red-earth paint. Between them upon their couch lay the well-wrapped roll of the thunder medicine. They purified themselves with sweetgrass smoke and began singing the four sacred songs of the medicine, we all singing with them. First was the song of Thunder Bird. Then came the buffalo song, the antelope song, and the wolf song. Oh, wonderful, intensely heart-stirring was that buffalo song; so solemn, deep-sounding, and slow of tune. In time to it we four times made the sign for buffaloes; four times with tightly closed hands imitated the heavy, slow walk of an old bull; and four times made the sign for a robe. It was really a song-prayer to the gods for ample sustenance; above all creatures the buffaloes were our food, our shelter, and our clothing.

More Discoveries

After each song was sung North Woman spread open a wrapping of the sacred medicine, and so after the fourth song it lay exposed to view, a long pipestem decorated with beautiful feathers, different furs, and bands of fine porcupine-quill work. Reverently the old man lifted it, pointed it to the sky, the ground, to the north, south, east, and west, and then made a long prayer to the gods for our long life, good health, and happiness, and an especial prayer to Thunder Bird in which he asked him to come often with his rains so that in due time the berry-bushes would bend low with their weight of ripe, sweet fruit, and our planting of nah-wak'-o-sis grow to a good harvest of large, strong leaves.

Following that the prayer the old man made for Dove Woman and me, entreating the gods to keep us safe from all dangers, and aid us to wipe out our enemy of the cañon, brought tears to our eyes. He prayed, too, for the quick healing of Long Bear's arm. He then danced around the fireplace four times, holding the sacred stem to the sky, and then my father danced with it, and I last, the women singing the Thunder-Bird dance-song for us. Following that Old Sun fitted a nah-wak'-o-sis-filled pipebowl to the stem, and the three of us smoked to the gods in turn, praying them to receive our smoke offering and to pity us all. And while we were doing that, the women set out before us and themselves and the children bowls of stewed service-berries. The pipe was laid away. We each lifted

The Dreadful River Cave

a hornspoonful of the berries to the gods, and begged them to pity us. We then dug little holes in the ground before us, dropped the berries into them and covered them, praying Earth, our great mother, to pity us. And then we ate the remaining berries, and so ended the ceremony of the Thunder-Bird medicine.

Dove Woman followed me out of the lodge to a seat upon a log in the warm sunshine. The women and children passed us and went on to the edge of our planting, sat all in a row facing it, and began to sing — so soft and low that we could no more than hear them:

> "Seeds of nah-wak'-o-sis, Thunder Bird
> Has come and brought you rain,
> Oh, plenty of rain to wet your feet.
> Seeds of nah-wak'-o-sis, grow! grow!
> Grow into large and perfect leaf!
> Grasshoppers, beware! Come not upon this
>   sacred ground!
> Sun, shine down; and come, more rain
> And help these seeds to perfect life!"

Over and over they sang the song, and how pleasant it was to our ears! Long Bear came and sat with us, and I said to my almost-sister, and signed to him: "Our prayers to Thunder Bird, how they have heartened me! I feel that he, that the sun himself, is with us! I now have fresh courage, greater courage than ever to watch for the person in the cañon, no matter what he is, water evil one or real person, and bring his life to a quick end."

More Discoveries

"That is just the way I feel, but let us never again watch in the night for him," said the girl.

"The next time you go to watch down there I go with you," Long Bear signed to us, and added, when he saw that I was about to object; "Don't refuse me. I must go with you. I shall be very careful not to injure my arm."

"We will go down there now," I said, and went for my weapons, and Dove Woman for the gun that she was carrying.

It was in my mind to see what had become of our bull carcass, and those of the bears, so I led the way down to them instead of straight to the falls. There were no fresh tracks on the rain-beaten trails of the meat-eaters converging at the carcasses, but great numbers of birds flew up from them at our approach. The bear carcasses, hugely swelled, were as we had left them; of the bull carcass there remained only the head and the gnawed and scattered bones.

The heaviest one of the trails of the meat-eaters led from the bull carcass straight down to the beaver pond. It was the trail that I had started by dragging the liver and lungs of the animal to the place of our first kill, the moose. I started to follow it, thinking that it would be well to have a look at the pond, when Dove Woman called my attention to the head of the bull. She came running to me, making the sign for silence, and whispered: "Its tongue is gone! Removed just as though some one had cut it out!"

The Dreadful River Cave

I hurried back to the head with her, Long Bear following us. The tongue was gone, but the lower jaw remained in place and tight-closed against the upper jaw. It did not seem possible that any animal, bear or wolf or any other kind, could have taken the tongue without tearing off the lower jaw with it. I knelt beside the head and turned it up. You know what we do when we cut out a tongue: just run a knife along the inner edge of the jawbone and sever its binding meat, then reach in and grasp the end of the tongue and pull it straight back and cut it off at its base. Well, I saw at once that the tongue had been cut out, and Dove Woman and Long Bear, leaning over the head on each side of me, were equally sure that it had been removed with a knife.

"Some enemy has been here!" I said as I sprang to my feet.

"Yes. The Under-Water person, of course," Dove Woman said.

"Be careful! That was knife work!" Long Bear signed to us.

We looked all around, made sure that no one was in sight, and then circled the place, the birds scolding down at us. They made us very uneasy. We circled the place not once, but four times, a larger circle each time, but found no signs of the tongue-stealer, and again striking the trail to the pond I led the way down it. Of one thing I was certain, and it gave me strength of heart: the gods had put

136

More Discoveries

it into my mind to go to our kills instead of straight to the falls, so that we should have warning that an enemy was somewhere near by. I prayed them to continue leading me; to help me to wipe out this enemy before he could discover our little camp, and had faith that they would do so.

We soon came to the end of the heavy trail, and from the shelter of the shore brush looked out upon the big beaver pond, instantly discovering that the top of the beaver lodge, from which we had watched our moose kill, had been torn apart and the sticks thrown into the water; they had been recently thrown in, for none of them had floated in to shore nor out far from the lodge.

"There! The enemy again! He was been spearing beaver!" Dove Woman exclaimed.

CHAPTER IX

NO. Just look up there and you will know who did it," I told her, and pointed to a lodge near the head of the pond. A big wolverine was on it, with paws and jaws and hard pressing-back, tearing the roof-sticks apart and pushing them off into the water. He was not doing that because he expected to tear his way into the lodge and capture one of the beavers, for he well knew that they would be gone from it before he could get the roof off. He was doing all that hard work because of the mean heart of him; he was the cruel joker of the mountains. Wandering about with full belly he still killed every small animal and bird that he could seize, and failing to kill he destroyed their dens and stores of food and their nests. And now he was tearing the roofs off the lodges of the beavers just to cause them a lot of trouble.

"Oh, the mean-faced, evil animal!" Dove Woman exclaimed when she saw him and what he was doing, and she pushed out through the brush and flapped her robe at him, and he sprang into the water and swam for the shore.

"Come back here, crazy one!" I told her.

"Well, that mean-face made me so angry I for-

138

We Flee from Our Enemies

got all about our enemy. Don't scold, I will be careful," she answered, and sneaked back into the brush and stood behind me.

"Oh, well, I think you did no harm; if the enemy had been about here we should not have seen the wolverine," I said, and led the way back past the bear carcasses and thence, well out from the pond and the swamp, toward the falls. We saw no tracks of game along our trail; after the long, cold rain all the thin-haired grass-eaters were no doubt lying in the sun to warm themselves.

At last we crept to our shelter behind the juniper brush, and when Long Bear looked through them down at the falls he started back, clapping hand to mouth to show his great surprise. And then he signed to us: "That black hole in the cliff is a place to fear. I believe that it is the home of some of the Under-Water People."

"We think that only one of them lives there," I signed.

He shook his head. "No, if one lives there, then there must be more," he signed. "They are people like us, except that they live in the water. We do not live alone, neither do they."

I made no answer to that, but thought about it for some time and made up my mind that he was right; that there probably was more than one of our enemies of the water in the river cave. That far-back, diving ancestor of ours who had visited in their deep-down lodges told upon his return that

The Dreadful River Cave

they loved their camp-life; that none ever went away upon lone and far wanderings.

After we had watched the falls and the big pool for some time, seeing no living thing but an otter, I proposed that we circle around and go on discovery beyond the falls, perhaps as far as the upper lake.

"You two go. I will remain here and watch the place for you," Long Bear signed.

I objected to that. "You have but one hand, and no weapon for it. If you were attacked you could not defend yourself; you would be quickly killed," I told him.

"No. See what you have done for me," he signed to us, looking at me and again at Dove Woman and happily smiling. "I was your enemy, but you gave me my life, brought me to your camp, and cared for me as though I was your own brother. And this day your medicine man prayed for me! Sun is my god as well as yours! I feel that he took that strong prayer, that he will protect me. I now want to do something for you. Go upon your trail of discovery and leave me to watch this place until you return."

Now, when he signed that he expressed my own thought. I, too, felt that Old Sun's prayers had been heard, that the gods were giving us protection. I therefore signed to him to remain where he was, and that we should return before sundown.

As we backed away from him he smiled again and took up a loose piece of rock. "There are plenty of them; they shall be my weapons. If any

We Flee from Our Enemies

one attacks me I shall with these knock him upon
his head," he signed.

We smiled back at him, signed to him to be wise
like the wolf, and got upon our feet and climbed
the steep cañon-side.

Dove Woman and I had never been upon the
cliff from the edge of which the lesser falls poured
down into the falls from the mouth of the river
cave. I now led the way to it and we soon came into
a heavy game trail that ran across it from the mountains upon one side of the valley to the mountains
on the other side. Old signs along it showed that
it was traveled mostly by bighorns and white goats.
I had noticed often that these dwellers upon the
bare, rocky heights of the mountains never failed
to make their valley crossings by the shortest and
least-timbered route, as this was, and that they
made their crossings on the swift run. They feared
the timber, or rather their enemies that it concealed.

The top of the cliff was thickly timbered except
along the narrow course of the stream, so narrow
where it made its first drop — to a shelf not far below — that we could jump across it. We did jump
it, and paused and looked off at the north side of
the cañon, and saw Long Bear's head and shoulders
where he sat behind the juniper brush. He was
much lower down than we, and not far away, just
about the distance of a long gun-shot. I waved to
him, and he waved his hand, and sank so low in his
hiding-place that we could no longer see him. He no

The Dreadful River Cave

doubt thought that he was exposing too much of his body to the view of any enemy that might appear.

We were about to go on up the stream when we discovered, almost at our feet, a small pile of stones; and we saw that they had recently been placed there, for some of them were partly coated with living moss that along its edges had fresh, straight break-offs. We stared down at the pile, wondering who had placed it there, and what was its meaning. I toed off the top of the pile, saw something white below, and stooped and took it up. Dove Woman sprang away from me when she saw what it was, and I was near dropping it: the thing that I held in my hand was a necklace of the joints of the backbone of a very large fish.

"Oh, what a bad-medicine thing! Put it back at once where you got it! Re-pile the stones!" the girl urged me, and I did so, but not until I had noticed that the string of the necklace was not leather nor sinew, but a braided substance that appeared to be grease-softened fish-skin.

"The Under-Water person, he of the cave beneath us, that is his necklace!" she said.

"Yes!" I answered. "No longer must we guess if he of the river cave, tracker of the sands, is a water enemy or one of our land enemies. This find proves that he is an Under-Water person. No other would wear a fish-bones necklace. And here he laid it, his sacrifice to his gods."

We Flee from Our Enemies

The girl was very uneasy; she looked all around, into the thick timber on each side of us, down into the cañon, and up the stream. "Let us get away from here!" she exclaimed.

I hesitated. "I am minded to take up that necklace again and keep it," I told her.

"Oh, no! Don't take it!" she pleaded. "Well you know that no one ever takes an enemy's sacrifice to his gods. You don't want to anger them, do you? Come, let us go."

"But his gods are not our gods; they are our enemies as well as he is," I argued, and stooped to take up the necklace.

"It will not fly away," she said, seizing my arm; "let it remain there until we can consult with your father and Old Sun about it."

"Well, have your way about it," I agreed and took the lead back across the stream and up along it, cautioning the girl to avoid stepping upon sandy and muddy places.

"You did n't have to tell me that! I am not a little child!" she hissed at me over my shoulder. I looked back at her and bit my lips to keep from laughing at her angry face. She was very proud of her warrior-hunter knowledge and hated to be cautioned.

We followed up the stream to the foot of the upper lake, on our way again stopping at the bed of big stones between which the greater part of the flow disappeared. It certainly was a medicine place.

The Dreadful River Cave

Winter and summer since most ancient time the stream had been sucked down there into the head of the long cave, yet the driftwood and gnawed beaver cuttings and dead leaves it carried had never choked the many small places of its disappearance. There was no doubt but Old Man had so fixed them that they could not be choked.

We found no fresh tracks of any kind along the stream, nor at the foot of the lake, and decided to go no farther up the valley. We seated ourselves upon a big flat rock at the outlet for a rest and a look at the mountain-slopes of the great valley.

Said Dove Woman: "Now, about that bull's tongue. I somehow can't think that the Under-Water person cut it out. It is more reasonable that we also have a land enemy here in the valley, and it was he who took it."

"The Under-Water People had plenty of dried meat as well as strawberries in their lodges when our diving ancestor visited them," I told her, shortly, for I was watching a band of white goats grazing low down upon the slope of the great red mountain that we faced, the mountain rising steeply from the north side of the lake and the stream. They were quite close to the edge of the timber. We could easily go up and kill one or two of them, and return to the falls for Long Bear and get home before sundown. I told the girl my plan and we began the climb.

My friend, you will know later on what might

We Flee from Our Enemies

have happened to us, to our little camp, if we had
not looked twice at the goats, and had gone straight
back to the falls. Mysterious are the ways of the
gods! How often, without our perceiving it at the
time, do they direct our steps for our protection!

' The mountain-slope was steep and well timbered.
We climbed slowly, often stopping to rest, for I did
not want to be out of breath when the time came
for me to shoot at the goats. I had my bow as well
as my gun with me, and hoped that I could get
close enough to the animals to use the noiseless
arrows. Our course was slanting northward up the
slope. From the time that we entered the timber
there was no possibility of our seeing the goats
again until we arrived at the upper edge of it, and
when, at last, we did look out from it we found that
the animals had turned about and were grazing
some distance north of where we had seen them,
but were still within bowshot of the timber. I was
about to draw back into the timber and keep on
until opposite them, when we saw them suddenly
raise their heads and stare at something below,
then turn and start off up the mountain as fast as
they could go. At the same time we heard the barking of dogs, then saw them in pursuit of the goats,
and after them five men, running faster up that
slope than I had ever seen men run upon level
ground. That alone proved who they were, big-
legged mountain men, of course, and of course our
enemies! I had often heard our warriors tell of the

The Dreadful River Cave

great size of the leg muscles of our mountain enemies, and their big-lunged bodies. It was even said that they could run up a mountain faster than we riders of the plains could run down it.

Just at that time we did not think much about ourselves, for we knew that the enemy had not discovered us, and that we could sneak quietly away whenever we chose to do so; we were too much interested in what was going on up on the open slope to move. The goats — seven of them and all old males — were heading for the near-by first cliff of the mountain, and the dogs, urged on by the shouts of the men, were gaining upon them, and surrounded and brought them to a stand before they were halfway to the cliff. They bunched up in a close circle, heads out, and the yelping dogs ran around and around them, but always at a safe distance from their sharp black horns. Then came the men with their bows and arrows and began shooting the white ones, and one by one they fell and died, and the dogs rushed in and tore at their bodies. But not for long; the men drove them off, then laid down their bows and recovered their arrows, and began skinning the animals. We sneaked back into the heavy timber.

And now it was time for us to do something and do it quick. I turned about and said to my almost-sister: "Well, at last the enemy has come into our valley; our little camp is in great danger. We have to learn if they are a war party passing through

We Flee from Our Enemies

the country, or if there is a big camp of them come in here to hunt."

"Yes. And also get Long Bear away from the falls," she said. "Go on; do what you think is best to do. I follow you."

I first wanted to know if the five men had horses or were afoot, so led on along the mountain-side and soon saw some horses tethered to the trees. We went close up to them, five big black-white horses, the kind that the River People[1] raised, and so knew who the goat-killers were. Oh, how I wanted those horses! There they stood, mine for the taking of them, and I had to leave them. That hurt!

We went on, back-tracking the horses, and at the eastern end of the red mountain came to the trail that they had left, the trail that runs up behind the big mountain to the head of Cutbank River, and then down the west side of the range. It was all cut up by the tracks of a great number of horses that had gone down it, big horses and little horses and colts, and in their tracks were here and there the tracks of dogs. How I had hoped that the goat-killers were a war party passing through the mountains; this big, fresh trail proved that they were hunters from an enemy tribe that had come across the mountains to steal some of our buffaloes. Camp would doubtless be made somewhere along the lower lake, and the men, scatter-

[1] The Kalispels.

The Dreadful River Cave

ing out to hunt, would some of them discover our camp. My heart almost went dead as I thought what then would happen!

"Almost-sister," I said, "this is terrible! Our people are in great danger! We must go to them as fast as we can run with the news of our discovery."

"We cannot leave Long Bear there at the falls; we must have him with us!" she answered.

"Of course. He is but a little way from here. Come, we will go to him," I told her, and away we went, not upon the trail to leave our footprints in it, but along its lower side.

This across-the-mountains trail joined the big valley trail at a point not far west of the falls, and it ran close by the falls, but not within sight of them. We hurried on, keeping a good lookout ahead, you may be sure, and turned down into the cañon when we heard the roar of the falls. And then we discovered that Long Bear was not there behind the juniper brush, where he was to remain until we returned for him! Our first thought was that he had been killed by some of the passing enemy. We sprang from shelf to shelf down the steep cañon-side to the hiding-place and found no signs of him, nor any blood upon the bare rocks. But that proved nothing; he might have run from the enemy until he was overtaken and killed. We could not stop to look for him. There was the chance that he had become tired of waiting for us and had gone back to camp. We were greatly worried about him, Dove

We Flee from Our Enemies

Woman especially. As we turned and climbed out of the cañon I heard her calling upon the gods to keep him safe from our mountain enemies.

The sun was near setting when we broke into camp with our bad news, and before we had half-told it the children were crying and old Red Wing Woman was interrupting us with her wails.

"You children, if you don't stop crying we shall give you to the enemy! And you, old woman, setting our ears afire with your talk, close your mouth at once or I shall give you to the sun!" Old Sun hissed to them.

"That is it! That is it! You got me up into this terrible country, and now you ask the gods to curse me!" the old woman cried.

Old Sun groaned. "I marvel that any one ever took you for a wife! You tongue-killed that man of yours! Yes, that is what you did, scolded him to death!" he told her.

"Oh, have done with this, both of you. Be ashamed of yourselves, quarreling at such a time — when the enemy is almost upon us!" my father cried.

And then I did complete what I had to say, and to ask for Long Bear, although I knew that was useless.

"We shall not see him again! I am sure that he is dead," said Dove Woman.

Her voice sounded so strange that I turned and looked at her. She had covered her face with her robe and was crying.

The Dreadful River Cave

"Ha! Whether alive or dead, that youth of the Spotted People is nothing to you!" Red Wing Woman scolded.

The girl did not answer her. I, myself, believed that our friend was dead.

"Well, one thing is sure: none of the hunters of these buffalo-stealers will be up here this evening," said my father, "but some of them will be hunting up along this ridge in the morning. Undoubtedly they will make camp somewhere just below the lake, where their horses will have good grazing upon the little valley prairies, and hunt mostly down the river. We have this night to move away from here, and I propose that we go down on Cutbank River and remain there until the enemy kill what buffaloes they want and go back whence they came."

"Hai-yo! All our work, all our prayers, all our sacrifices were for nothing: the enemy will destroy our sacred planting!" Old Sun mourned.

"Don't talk so foolishly!" my father told him. "How can they destroy the nah-wak'-o-sis when it has not come up in sight? We will take down our lodges and hide the lodgeskins, and all else that we cannot take with us upon our two horses; and so, leaving nothing here to attract their attention, it is more than likely that the wandering hunters will not even see our planting-place."

The old man took courage at that and straightened up and addressed the women. "You are all

We Flee from Our Enemies

of you frightened and excited; just calm yourselves; think what you have to do and then do it carefully. But first give us something to eat, and yourselves eat plenty, for we have a long night of work and travel ahead of us," he told them.

Well, as soon as we finished eating, Dove Woman and I went for the two horses and saddled them, and first packed off into the brush and hid here and there the many riding- and pack-saddles that we had. Then the moon came up and we had plenty of light for packing off and hiding the lodgeskins and the many parfleches and sacks of the belongings of our three families. But it was not near midnight when we finished that work and loaded the horses with the things that we were to take with us, the sacred medicines, some dried meat, some buffalo robes, and trailed out of our well-cleared camp-ground.

' Up we went to the top of the ridge, and down its north slope to the fork of Cutbank River, and thence to its junction with the main stream. We were obliged to travel more and more slowly on account of the tired and sleepy children that were too large to be carried, so did not strike the main river until after daylight, and the sun was well up before we found, below, a large, dense thicket of willows in which to make our lodgeless camp. We went well into the center of the growth, unsaddled and picketed the horses, and all lay down and fell asleep.

The Dreadful River Cave

It was a restless and short sleep that we had; we were not accustomed to sleeping in the daytime, and, too, our minds were full of anxious thoughts. The women were very sad-faced and quiet as they built a fire and roasted some dried meat for us, all but Red Wing Woman, who loudly grumbled about our bad luck, and kept foretelling worse to come, until, to our surprise, my always gentle mother turned upon her and gave her a scolding that she would not soon forget. As soon as she became quiet I told my father and Old Sun of our discovery of the fish-bones necklace, and they both said that they were glad I had not taken it, for it undoubtedly was the Under-Water person's offering to his evil gods, and so would have brought bad luck to me.

Oh, we had much to talk about that morning! We wondered what had been poor Long Bear's end, how long the enemy would remain in the Two Medicine Valley, and if they would find any of the property that we had cached. We talked, too, of the chances of our being discovered where we were by a passing war party, and my father cautioned the women and children to keep close in the brush and to make no noise. We decided that from dawn until night we would keep daily watch upon the country for approaching enemies, and if any were discovered move up or down the river or remain right where we were, as the need might be. Right north of us a steep hill stood at the edge of the timbered

We Flee from Our Enemies

valley. Dove Woman and I went up on it to watch until late afternoon, when my father and mother would take our places.

We sat between growths of sagebrush and looked off at the great plain, to the north sloping up to the bare ridge of Little River, and southward up to the higher and timbered ridge of the Two Medicine. We could see nothing to indicate that enemies were about; everywhere the buffaloes and antelopes were quietly resting and grazing. I somehow felt that we might sit there all summer and discover not one war party.

I looked at my almost-sister, sitting somewhat back of me, strangely silent and sad of face: "You are grieving for Long Bear; you must have thought very much of him," I said.

"I did," she answered. "Never, never was there a braver, more good-hearted youth than he; so cheerful in all his suffering, too. I was making a pair of moccasins for him, and now he will never wear them!" And with that she began to cry.

"Take courage! We don't know that he is dead; he may yet return to us," I told her, just to cheer her up. I felt sure that his scalped body was lying somewhere near the falls.

"Oh, if I could only believe that! I will believe it!" she said. And she did take courage, and drew from under her robe the moccasin uppers that she was embroidering with porcupine quills and resumed work upon them.

The Dreadful River Cave

"It was my intention to bury them here upon this hill. But now I shall finish making them, praying with every quill I lay that he will soon see my work," she said.

The day wore on. In the late afternoon, when my father and mother came up to relieve us, I told him at once what I had been thinking during our long watch.

"This is no place for me," I said. "Were the enemy to come I could not save you from them; you would all be wiped out or all escape their notice, and I should be just one more to die with you or survive with you. The thing for me to do is to go back to the Two Medicine and watch those buffalo-stealers, and come for you as soon as they move away."

"Well, you need n't be so fire-tongued about it, for that is just what we expect you to do," my father answered.

"Good. I shall go to-night," I told him.

"And I go with you!" Dove Woman exclaimed.

"Absolutely not! Upon this danger trail I go alone," I told her.

"Of course not! Daughter, we need you here to watch for us; our eyes are none too good," my father told her.

She knew that we meant it and did not once plead to have her way, which considerably surprised me. I feared that she intended to sneak off upon my trail.

We Flee from Our Enemies

And then I saw that I was wrong, for when my father said that I could not leave until I had killed some meat, she told him she would kill all that could be used.

Soon after sunset, with gun and bow, and upon my back a small sack of dried meat and dried fat, I crossed the river and struck off over the plain upon my lone adventure. My father and Old Sun had prayed for my safe return. I felt strong for my undertaking.

CHAPTER X

WHEN I arrived at the top of the Two Medicine ridge — at a point away to the east of our camp-ground upon it — the Seven Persons[1] marked the middle of the night. I hurried down the slope to the foot of the lake and the big trail crossing of the outlet, and found, as I expected, that the enemy had there gone over to the other side of the stream. I took off my moccasins and leggings and forded, dressed as quickly as I could, and took up their trail across the little valley prairie, easy to follow in the bright moonlight. It ran straight through the second prairie and then up onto the level, half-timber and half-prairie point between the river and its south fork. I then heard what I had been listening for, the barking of dogs, and presently saw the camp of the enemy and counted their lodges, twenty-two of them, all in a row at the edge of a grove of pines. In between and in front of them were picketed horses, the fast buffalo-runners, of course, and out in the open, grazing as they willed, were the bands of common animals. Here was a chance for me in one night to make myself rich. Just imagine how upside down I felt that

[1] The Big Dipper.

I Trick the Enemy and They Flee

I could not take it! If I ran off a band of the fine mountain horses I should have to keep going until I could strike our big camp at the Point-of-Rocks River, and there leave them with our relatives. I told myself that I must not even think about it; that my one duty was to watch the enemy out of the country, and then get our little camp back to our nah-wak'-o-sis planting.

I turned off into the timber and stole silently through it to the camp. It was red with drying meat; the hunters had made a big killing of buffaloes — our buffaloes. My heart was all on fire at them. I asked myself what I could do to punish them — to drive them out of the country?

Ha! Behind one of the lodges, upon its red-painted willow tripod, were suspended a medicine man's sacred belongings, his well-wrapped pipe-stem, two painted and fringed pouches full of various things, and his shield in its leather covering. I said to myself that I would take them, tripod and all, and thus destroy his power. Without his medicine his prayers would be of no avail; fear would fill the hearts of his people; they would break camp and go back into their own country.

I went out to the tripod — it was but a few steps from the timber — and was about to take it up with all its hangings, when I saw the long fringe of one of the pouches begin to sway and flutter slightly as though wind-blown. But there was no wind; no, none at all! I backed away from the tripod as fast

The Dreadful River Cave

as I could without making any noise, and turned into the timber. Well I knew what had caused that fringe to flutter: the shadows of the medicine man's gods were protecting the sacred things. I shivered when I thought of what might have happened to me had I even touched them: medicine shadows had the power to give people strange and painful diseases which were incurable!

I had examined but six lodges of the camp. I soon took courage to go on and look at the rest. I sneaked along the edge of the timber and came close behind the tenth lodge, a very large and new one of white leather and strangely painted with a circle of black animals the like of which I had never seen or heard of; their heads were shaped like that of a dog, but their bodies were without legs and ended like the tail of a fish. I wondered what kind of medicine the owner of this lodge had. I could see only the back of it and was curious to see its front side. I was not afraid of the dogs; some of them had already been smelling at my heels. I looked long and carefully all up and down the length of the camp, saw nothing suspicious, and started out from the timber.

There were two horses picketed between the painted lodge and the next lodge on its left, and one horse between it and the lodge on its right. I went out by the lone horse, lying down and sound asleep, noticing as I passed that he was a very fine black-white animal, very large, big-muscled, and

I Trick the Enemy and They Flee

fat. His picket rope was not fastened to a stake; it ran in under the skin of the painted lodge and was undoubtedly tied to the bed-rail of the owner, who had only to reach out and pull in the slack to know that his valuable racer was still safely fastened to the other end of it, not all tangled up in it, leg-burned and perhaps choking, as frequently happens when high-spirited, nervous horses are put upon a rope.

Well, I sneaked out in front of that lodge and was turning to look at it when that black-white horse awoke and became suddenly frightened, no doubt at my slow and stealthy movements. He sprang to his feet, loudly snorting, and tried to run off, fetching his rope taut with such a fierce jerk that it tore the lodgeskin up from its pegs. I started to run past him back into the timber, and did advance a few leaps when I saw that in his wild circling he was likely to trip me with the rope. I therefore turned to run around the front of the lodge and past its other side. I wanted to get back into the timber as quickly as possible — instead of running off across the moonlit prairie and be chased by all the men of the camp. Already the women and children of the lodge were making great outcry, and as I was about to pass the doorway a man sprang out from it with an arrow-fitted bow in his hands. I was expecting just that and was holding my gun ready for the attack; before he could straighten up from his leap through the doorway

159

The Dreadful River Cave

and take aim at me, I fired straight at his breast and he fell sprawling at my feet. I snatched up his bow and ran on around the lodge and into the timber, sure that I had not been seen by any of the men of the camp as they shouted to one another and rushed from their lodges. Oh, how happy, how proud of myself I was! I had counted *coup* upon an enemy! The bow in my hands was proof of it! I fairly hugged that bow, determined that, if need be, I would throw away my gun rather than let go of it!

I went on through the timber, westward past the camp, and then again to the edge of it and looked out upon the prairie. As I thought they would do, the men were rounding up their horse herds and driving them in to the lodges. I fired my gun up then and raised the war song of my people. My bullet had no effect upon them, but I am sure that the song did; they had often heard it and always to their sorrow; even then the wailing of the women of the painted lodge was in their ears. They knew that they had been discovered in their buffalo-stealing raid, but they could not know that the discoverer was a lone youth of their terrible enemy, the Pi-kun'-i. In my natural voice I shouted: "Did you kill the one you fired at?" and in a deep voice shouted the answer: "Yes, I killed him and took his bow!" And in still another voice: "That is good, my friend!" And so on in imitation of the voices of a number of men. And fired again and again at the

I Trick the Enemy and They Flee

enemy. Oh, it was good to see them rounding their horses with all the haste that they could make. I was quite sure that they would break camp at daylight, and go back across the mountains into their own country, not upon the trail by which they had come, but by the easier and more direct trail running up the South Fork of the Two Medicine. But there I was, shouting and shooting, pretending to be a big war party between them and the trail. Back into the timber I went, circled around to the east of their camp, and fired my gun and shouted and sang. But not for long; daylight was coming. I sneaked off into the timber, crossed the river, and from the high and brushy ridge to the east of it sat down to see what I should see. Day came. With the rising of the sun the buffalo-stealers formed into column, and I was surprised to see so many riders; there must have been three or four hunters and their families in every lodge. Twenty or thirty scouts took the lead and rode off to the south-west to strike the big trail; they passed out of sight into the South Fork Valley, and then the long procession of riders and loose horses set out after them. As soon as they, too, passed out of sight, I lay down right where I was and slept until the middle of the day.

It was hunger that awoke me. I went down to the river and bathed, ate some dried meat, and considered going up to our camp-ground on the ridge to see if the enemy had discovered it and our

The Dreadful River Cave

various caches of property. I thought, too, about Long Bear, lying dead somewhere up near the falls, and grieved for him. He had become a real friend. And then I thought about the Under-Water person. I was determined to have it out with him without waste of time. To go now up to the campground would be waste of time, I said to myself. I finished eating and struck up over the ridge straight toward our brush camp on Cutbank River. Well I knew that in crossing the plain in the daytime I was running some risk, but I somehow felt strong to do it. Bands of buffaloes and of antelopes fled before me, but I took no heed of that. It was my medicine that was leading me on and giving me constantly the feeling that no enemies had their eyes upon my progress. Without having seen anything to alarm me I arrived at Cutbank River at sundown and hurried into our camp in the brush. I was expected. Dove Woman had descended from her watch upon the hill with the news that I was near, and all were waiting for my coming. I held up my enemy bow before them and cried: "I have killed an enemy! Behold his bow! I seized it when he fell at my feet!"

Ha! How they all crowded around me, praising my name, giving thanks to the gods for what I had done! And then, when my father had commanded quiet, I told all that I had seen and done over in the valley of the Two Medicine. I had barely finished when Old Sun began calling out to his women

I Trick the Enemy and They Flee

to pack up; that we would at once back-trail to our camp-ground upon the ridge.

"Go now if you will; myself, I shall eat, and have some sleep before I start for there!" I told him.

And my father said to him: "My friend, do have a little sense in your old age! We shall remain right here until my son is rested, and ready to lead us!"

We still had a little dried meat; it had not been necessary for Dove Woman to make a kill. I ate plenty, slept for a time, and before midnight we were upon our way back to the Two Medicine, Dove Woman and I in the lead.

"Almost-brother, you omitted to tell us how the front of that medicine lodge was painted," she said to me.

"For good reason: I never got to see it; just as I was turning to look at it the medicine man jumped out at me," I answered.

"His last jump! Oh, how proud I am of your *coup!*"

"Think how the gods protect us," I told her. "They put it into our minds, that day at the upper lake, to sit upon the flat rock and rest, and thus to discover to us the enemy."

"I have thought about it, oh, many times!" she exclaimed. "But, oh, if they had only warned Long Bear, too! Poor Long Bear!"

"Ai! Poor dead friend! He had n't our medicine," I said, and saw that she was crying.

Day was breaking when we went over the top of

The Dreadful River Cave

the ridge and approached our camp-ground. And then Old Sun suddenly got back — for the time — the legs of his youth: he ran swiftly on past us to our garden place, looked at it in the bright moonlight, and came dancing back, crying out to us: "The enemy never touched the place! Much of the nah-wak'-o-sis has broken up through the earth into the light! What happiness! What happiness!"

And then we heard the patter of other running feet, and looked to the west and saw — we could hardly believe our eyes — Long Bear running toward us and crying brokenly: "My friends! My friends!" Two of our words that he had learned.

Then was our happiness truly complete. Dove Woman ran to meet him; hung to his sound arm and led him to us, and right there we all sat down and had a sign talk with him, learned all that he had done, and I explained where we had been, and how I had counted *coup* upon the enemy and frightened them out of the country. Said Long Bear:

"After you left me there at the falls, I watched for a long time and saw nothing but an otter. I was lying down, got tired of that position, and sat up. As I did so I looked up, and there at the edge of the cañon was a rider, looking down at me! I saw him turn and shout and beckon to others, somewhere farther back, and as he dismounted from his horse I was going from there as fast as I could run down behind the rock point and across the not-deep

I Trick the Enemy and They Flee

rapids of the river. I looked back; three men were upon my trail. Before I could get into the timber they were firing arrows at me, but I was not hit. I got safely into the timber and ran on and on down toward the beaver pond, and when not far from it I stopped and looked back; the enemy were not in sight, nor could I hear them. I went into some thick brush and sat down.

"I sat there a long time. The enemy did not appear upon my trail, so I thought that they were scattered along the river, expecting that I would return to it. I wanted to go back to camp and tell you that the enemy had come into the valley, but was afraid that the enemy would see me and follow me. I stopped right where I was until the middle of the night, then went down along the beaver pond and crossed the river below it. When I came to the big trail and saw that many riders had gone down it, I hurried on up the ridge to tell you that a great camp of the enemy had come into the valley. I came here and found that you were gone, lodges and all. I looked around and could see no dead bodies, no signs of a fight. I knew that you could not move camp with two horses. I circled around and around, came first upon your cache of saddles, then a lodge-skin, robes, and some parfleches. Then I knew that you, too, had discovered the enemy, and that you would return as soon as it was safe for you to do so. I have remained right out there at the second cache I found, sleeping on the robes, eating some of the

The Dreadful River Cave

dried meat that was in one of the parfleches. Yesterday morning four of the enemy rode up by here, but not near enough to discover this camp-ground and your planting of smoking-leaves seed. Had your lodges been standing, had you all been here, think what would have happened!"

"It is plain enough what would have happened," my father said. "One of the four would have gone for all the men of their camp, the others would have watched us until they came, and then we should all have been wiped out."

"But we survive; the gods are with us; my medicine seems to tell me that we shall continue to survive all dangers. And now, you women, you know what there is to be done. Hurry! Do it! Let us have some comfort here!" cried Old Sun.

But, of course, before bringing out our caches and putting up the lodges we all had to go to the garden place and see the yellow-white heads of nah-wak'-o-sis that had broken up through the black, warm earth. There were hundreds of them in sight, a sight that made us all very happy. My father raised his hands and gave thanks to the gods; prayed them to continue protecting us from all dangers. And then we hurried away to our work, leaving him and Old Sun to smoke in peace there at the garden-side.

We soon had the lodges up and everything in place within them. The sun was well up by that time, so we built no fires and had just plain dried

I Trick the Enemy and They Flee

meat and backfat for our morning meal. My mother then proposed that I go out and kill a good supply of meat.

"I shall do no hunting this day," I told her. "I shall rest for a time, and then again watch at the falls for that Under-Water person!"

It was about the middle of the day when we arrived at our watching-place on the cañon-side, Dove Woman, Long Bear, and I, and looked down through the juniper brush at the falls. Not a living thing was in sight; not even a bird. It seemed to me that the falls were roaring more loudly than ever. There was certainly more water pouring from the top of the cliff than when we last had been at the place. Its spray almost entirely hid from us the black hole in the cliff from which the greater part of the river came foaming and roaring down into the deep pool.

More than once I had vowed that I would go into the cave and attack the Under-Water person if I found him there; but now, when the time was come for me to do it, my whole body suddenly turned as cold as the ice upon the mountain-tops. I looked at the powerful stream leaping from the darkness down its steeply slanting, boulder-strewn bed; were it to sweep me off my feet I would likely be so badly bruised and torn by the rocks that I should die. And if I safely made the ascent into the cave, what chance would there be for me — feeling my way along — against an enemy looking out at

The Dreadful River Cave

me from the darkness. Ha! At the thought of what might then happen, I shivered.

"Why are you shivering? The day is very warm. Are you sick?" Dove Woman asked.

"Sick at heart! My courage leaves me!" I cried. "I have more than once vowed to myself that I would go into that black hole and attack the enemy if I should find him there. Absolutely I cannot do it to-day."

"You shall never go in there! It is too dangerous an undertaking!" she exclaimed. "We have the whole summer before us. We will keep watch at this place until we see the enemy down there at the falls, and then we will wipe him out without danger to ourselves."

I made no answer to that, but decided that we would watch the place for a few days, and then, if we failed to see the cave-dweller, I would conquer my fear and go into the black hole in search for him.

We lay there in the warm sunlight a long time, seeing nothing but the leaping water, hearing nothing but its roar; the otters and minks, and even the little wading-birds seemed to have deserted the pool, and not a trout broke its whirling, heaving surface. At last the sun neared his lodge in the west. He went from our sight behind the great mountain and the first shadows of night stole out across the valley. It was time for us to go to our lodge. I was about to give the word when we saw a large black bear slowly walking up the far shore of the stream.

I Trick the Enemy and They Flee

When he arrived at the upper end of the big pool and was almost at the edge of the spray of the falls, he stopped short and took up something — we could not tell what — from a flat rock near the water, and hastily chewed and swallowed it, then nosed around among the rocks for more of the food. Finding none, he sat up straight upon his haunches and sniffed the air, and after some time got down upon all fours and began climbing the steep, rocky slant at the edge of the falls. He passed through the spray from the upper fall, and in the dusk we almost at once lost sight of him; but still we watched, saying nothing, and after a little time saw him come rolling and struggling down in the foaming water and disappear in the black depths of the pool. Then up he came, some distance out from the fall, and swam swiftly to the shore that he had left, and as soon as he struck it he went bounding up the steep cañon-side and out of our sight into the pines at the top of the slope.

"There! We now have proof enough that the enemy is in the cave!" I said and signed to my companions. "And how he frightened that black bear!"

"Ha! He went up that rocky steep as fast as he came tumbling down the falls. He surely was terribly frightened," said Dove Woman.

"We will remain here a little while longer; the enemy may now come out," I said.

But we did not see him, although we watched

The Dreadful River Cave

for him until the falls became only a dim, white blur in the darkness. And then we crawled back from our hiding-place and got upon our feet and hurried home as fast as we could make our way through the blackness in the timber. It was not pleasant going; our hearts were full of fear of we knew not what. An angry old bear might pounce upon us; Under-Water People were possibly trailing us; shadows of dead and gone enemies were perhaps hovering about, seeking to implant in our bodies a dreadful, incurable sickness. I can't begin to tell you how relieved we felt when, at last, we saw close ahead our lodges, glowing yellow-red with the light of the little fires within them. All out of breath and wet with perspiration we hurried into my father's lodge, where we found him smoking with Old Sun, and as shortly as I could I told them about the black bear — his going up into the river cave and his wild rush to get away from it.

"Ha! Undoubtedly the black sticky mouth smelled — and probably saw — the Under-Water person," said Old Sun. "I have often wondered what were the relations of the Under-Water People with the animals of the plains and forest. I thought that they might, perhaps, be friendly. Now I know: they are enemies."

"Son," my father said to me, "I wish you would cease watching for that cave-dweller. He is doing us no harm by his presence there, so it is best that he be left there in peace. You must remember that

I Trick the Enemy and They Flee

the Under-Water People have terrible power; far
more power than any of us who walk the earth.
Since Old Man made this world and put us Blackfeet here upon it, none of us have ever killed an
Under-Water person, but, oh, how many of us they
have dragged down to death in the deep waters!
It is true that I encouraged you to seek this
dweller in the river cave, but I have now changed
my mind. What our fathers — some of them medicine men of great power — have failed to do, you,
boy that you are, cannot hope to accomplish. I
say to you again: leave this enemy to live his
cold and watery life in peace."

"Oh, my son! As you love me, heed the request
of your wise father!" my mother cried.

"What you ask you ask too late. I have vowed
to the gods that I will seek this Under-Water person and try to kill him!" I told them.

And at that my father sank back in his seat with
a groan, and my mother and almost-mothers began
to cry. But Old Sun straightened up, swelled out
his breast, and with a loud clap of his hands exclaimed in thunder voice: "Because we and our
fathers before us have failed to do a certain thing
is not proof that it cannot be done. There has to be
a first time for everything. Friends all, my medicine seems to tell me that this your son is to accomplish that which he has set out to do. Anyhow,
having made his vow he cannot now go back on it,
his sacred promise to the gods. It is for us to help

The Dreadful River Cave

him all we can. Bear Eagle, dear friend, to-morrow you and I must again make medicine for him."

"Ai! We will do it. It is as you say: having made his vow, he must try to fulfill it," my father answered.

"Well," said my mother, as she dried her tears and motioned Little Fox Woman to set food before us, "to-morrow will be one day that he will not be risking his life in search of that old cave-dweller: this camp is out of meat!"

"Meat you shall have and plenty of it," I told her.

CHAPTER XI

AGAIN THE ENEMY

AT daybreak Long Bear and I had our bath in the little outlet of the spring. We returned to the lodge, and Dove Woman came in and combed and braided his hair and painted his face. She loved to wait upon him. We had a poor meal of scraps of meat. I begged for some of the pemmican that I knew my mother had, but she would give us none of it. It was, she said, a reserve of food against a time of trouble. As soon as we finished eating, Dove Woman and I brought in and saddled the horses, and she upon one, and Long Bear upon the other with me, we started out for meat. I wanted to go out to the edge of the plain and kill one or two buffaloes, but the risk of being discovered by some passing enemy was too great. I headed for the upper lake and the heavily timbered stream putting into it from the southwest. I was sure that we should there find plenty of elk — perhaps some moose.

We crossed the big trail to the West and Dove Woman got down and brushed out our horses' tracks upon it, and then we crossed the above-ground stream of the Two Medicine just back of the falls. It was all I could do to go on without a look down at them for a sight of the Under-Water

The Dreadful River Cave

person, but I again called out to the sun that I would seek him in his dark cave some time before the beginning of the Berries-Ripe Moon, and that was some satisfaction. Dove Woman, hearing me, cried out: "Oh, almost-brother! Now you have done it! You have set the time for your terrible adventure! Oh, how I fear for you!"

Long Bear, sensing a word or two of our talk, signed that he wanted to know all about it, and I told him.

"I am greatly disappointed. I had hoped that you would not go into the cave until my arm became well and strong and I could go in with you," he signed.

And then Dove Woman laughed and clapped her hands and signed to the crippled one: "I was not mistaken! All the time I have been feeling that you would be wanting to do that! I am proud of you, almost-brother!"

"No. Not your almost-brother, your true friend is what I am," he signed. And I, looking over my shoulder at the girl, saw her turn her head away from him and red come into her smooth and beautiful face. I had my thoughts, but said nothing, and urged the horse onward into the timber.

There were some small prairies running from the foot of the lake down along the border of the stream, and these we avoided, keeping in the timber to the south of them, but not so far in that we could not see them. In the second one of the high-

Again the Enemy

grass openings we discovered three buffalo bulls, and I told Dove Woman that I was minded to kill them and end our hunt right there.

"Don't do it!" she said. "See the winter hair still covering their backs; they are old, and of such poor and tough flesh that our old people could never chew it."

"They may live for the present. If we fail to get good meat up the valley, then must their tongues and ai'-is-su-is-iks [1] be our evening and morning food," I answered.

Then Long Bear rode up beside us, signed "Many bighorns!" and pointed to the great red mountain across the river.

Sure enough, there were many of them, five different bands feeding upon the open, steep slopes of the mountain, one of the bands — of forty or fifty head — so low down that it was no more than a long gunshot from the foot of the lake. But we could never have seen even those nearest us had it not been for the large, round patches of white hair upon the hind end of their bodies. All but that part of them was of a grayish brown color that blended with the rocks and brush and grasses of the mountain-side. We saw not even an outline of their heads and bodies, nothing but those round white patches of hair appearing and disappearing, and again quickly flashing in sight as the animals

[1] Ai-is-su-is-iks: The dorsal or hump ribs of the buffalo. Always tender in even the poorest of the animals.

kept turning one way and another as they grazed. It was true, what our ancient people said, that Old Man had done the bighorns great wrong, when, after giving them an almost invisible coat of hair, he painted a great white circle upon their rumps that, when they moved, could be seen by the hunter from far distances.

"Yes. There is plenty of meat, good fat meat, across there," I signed to our friend, " but from all up and down this great valley it is in sight of any enemies who may be passing through here. We will hunt no more in open country unless hunger compels us to it."

"You are right. Quite right. I did not think that you would go up there after the bighorns. I only wanted you to see how many they were," he signed back to me.

We rode on through the timber, following a game trail that ran not far back from the shore of the lake, and came to the long, slender point running far out into it. There we picketed our horses and went on afoot, I in the lead, bow and arrows in hand, Dove Woman close following me with both her gun and mine, and Long Bear trailing after us, and carefully shielding his bandaged arm with his one good hand.

After passing the point we found that the game trails became more and more plentiful as we neared the mouth of the stream coming down the long valley to the southwest. As plentiful as are the

threads in a spider's web, so were the trails of elk
and moose and deer there in that forest of pine. I
led on very slowly, at each step expecting to see
some of the animals close ahead, but, strangely
enough, we at last arrived at the edge of the stream
without having had sight of a living thing, not even
a bird. Close in front of us was Rising Bull Mountain, timbered a little way up its lower slope, and
then thrusting its almost straight, rocky sides far
up into the blue. Here and there upon its cliffs were
white goats, some resting, some feeding, but, as I
said to Dove Woman, rather the tough meat of the
old buffalo bulls than their coarse meat, strong
with the odor and taste of musk. True, I did want
two or three of the thick-furred goatskins for my
couch, but there would be all the long summer in
which to get them.

I chose not to cross the little stream, and led the
way up along it, following a game trail so much
used, so hard-packed, that the sharp-pointed hoofs
of the animals made no dents in its surface. I noticed that all the red-willow bushes bordering it had
been stripped of their tender shoots; they were the
favorite food of moose and elk. I led on more slowly,
more cautiously than ever, for I felt that, where
so many animals had been trailing about and feeding during the night, some of them would be near by.
We had followed the trail but a little way when it
brought us to the top of a very steep rise of ground,
sparsely timbered, at the foot of which was a nar-

row, treeless, high-grassed strip of prairie that in the long ago had been a beaver pond. In its center was a large spring surrounded with a belt of bushes — thick growing willows about the height of a man, and as we stood looking down upon them we saw some at the outer left edge of the belt suddenly quiver. We could not see what it was that caused them to do so, but we knew: an animal of some kind, probably a horned animal, was lying under them and shaking his head at the flies that bothered him.

"Meat! Some kind of good meat is under those willows," I said to Dove Woman. And just then we saw three more quiverings of the willows in different parts of the belt. I was glad. I turned about and said and signed to my companions: "A whole band of hoofed animals is resting in there. Come you with me down to the edge of the timber, and then I will go on with my bow and arrows and kill some of them."

"I shall go on with you and shoot one of them," Dove Woman declared.

"No! We will make no gun thunder in this valley until we just have to shoot," I told her, and she made a face at me and tossed her head, and turned away.

"Oh, well, as you are so anxious to draw blood, here! take you my bow and arrows and do the killing!" I growled at her.

She whirled about and faced me, her eyes flash-

Again the Enemy

ing, and said: "You know I can't do that; you know I have n't the strength nor the skill to use your bow! You are just as mean as you can be! Always wanting to do all the killing yourself! One gunshot would not — "

She never finished what she was going to say, for just then she half-turned and saw Long Bear looking at her, oh, how grieved, how pityingly! And at that her anger left her as suddenly as it had come. With tears in her eyes she turned again and ran to me, crying, "Oh, what a bad girl I am! Pity me, almost-brother! I will be good," and kissed me lightly.

"Hush! You will frighten the game! It is nothing. You are my dear almost-sister," I told her.

But as I led on down the hill I felt somewhat hurt. Never before had Dove Woman spoken cross words to me. I did not deserve them. It was far more pleasure for me to see her kill game than it was to kill it myself; were it not that I feared the sound of her gun would perhaps be heard by a passing war party, I would let her shoot all the game that was needed in our three lodges.

We soon arrived at the foot of the slope and the edge of the timber; we looked out at the willows encircling the spring and saw them again quiver in several places: the game was still lying in them. I motioned to my companions to remain right where they were, and got down upon my hands and knees and went crawling out through the high prairie

179

The Dreadful River Cave

grass. I held my bow and an arrow in my left hand, and with my mouth kept firm grip upon four more arrows. What little wind there was came down the valley straight in my face. I thought that, by moving very slowly and silently, I could get very close to the game, shoot my first arrow into one of the animals right where they lay, kill another as it was getting upon its feet, and still another as the survivors started to run from me.

It was not far from the timber to the willows, probably no more than a hundred steps. When I had crawled about halfway to them I heard, back whence I had come, the hooting of an owl.

"It is strange that an owl should be hooting in the daytime; this may mean bad luck for me," I said to myself, and listened for it to hoot again, which it did almost at once, and my ears told me that it was no owl that was doing the hooting. Dove Woman or Long Bear was taking that way to attract my attention, and still not alarm the game, lying ahead of me in the willows. I slowly straightened up until I was head and shoulders above the thick grass, and looked back at them: both were pointing out into the little prairie, at a place midway between the willows and the stream, and looking that way I could see the tall grass ripple as something moved slowly through it toward the willows. It was, I thought, a cougar or a wolf on the trail of the game that was lying in them. I became angry. I did n't intend to be cheated out

Again the Enemy

of my discovery. I dropped back upon hands and knees and went on as fast as I could crawl, not toward the willows, but to the right of them to intercept the approaching trailer, whatever it was, and frighten it away. It was twice as far from the willows as I was, so I was sure that I should have time to do so before it could get near enough to the game to alarm it. Nevertheless, I hurried, crawling faster than I ever had before, and upon arriving in front of the lower side of the belt of willows and twenty-five or thirty steps out from them, came upon the trail, by no means a plain one; just a crushing of the tall grass here and there where the animals had walked through it. There I sat up, my back to the willows, and fitted an arrow to my bow. I sat up straighter and could see close ahead the rippling of the grass as the trailer forced its way through it right toward me. I sank back and made ready to shoot.

Then fear suddenly came upon me: What if the trailer was an enemy? Worse than that, a real bear? I made a move to spring to my feet and run from that approaching rippler of the grass. But no! I could not do that! What — run from a thing I had not seen, prove myself a coward before my almost-sister and Long Bear? No. I would stop right there and face it, whatever it was. I called upon the sun for help; for strength of heart and arms. I begged that I might survive all the dangers that lurked in the great valley. As I finished my silent prayer I

The Dreadful River Cave

heard a faint rustling of the grass; saw the tall stalks parting, bending right and left where the trailer was thrusting its way through them. And then, not two steps in front of me, appeared the trailer, a big, yellow-eyed cougar. So great was my relief that almost I laughed in his face! I was holding my bow in readiness. I drew back the strung arrow quickly, with all my strength, aiming it fair at the white-pointed breast so near me, and let it fly. It sank in through skin and flesh and heart almost to the end of the feathering, and the big seizer sprang straight up, high above the top of the grass, and came down where he had stood with a loud thud. He gasped for breath; his sharp-clawed feet ripped the heavy grass up by the roots and flung moist, black earth into my face. Ha! As I shielded my eyes from it I heard behind me the thud of heavy feet, the loud snap of a dry stick. I whirled about where I sat and saw a big bull moose lunge out almost clear from the willows and stop, and with quick jerks of his head look for the cause of the noise that he had heard. I did not want to risk a shot at his thick-meated, heavy-boned breast. I hoped that he would turn side to me. He did, and with the utmost strength of my arms I sent my arrow deep into it, low down, and just back of the shoulder. He whirled about and crashed back into the willows, and as I sprang to my feet and ran after him, three other bulls broke from cover and trotted swiftly off across the little prairie and

AND THEN, NOT TWO STEPS IN FRONT OF ME, APPEARED
THE TRAILER, A BIG, YELLOW-EYED COUGAR

Again the Enemy

away from my companions, who were hurrying toward me.

I found my bull dead at the edge of the spring. He was the largest moose that I had ever seen, and I could tell by his rounding hip that he had already taken on some summer fat. Dove Woman and Long Bear came running through the brush to me, and were very happy when they saw the dead moose.

"And the big seizer — we saw him leap high above the grass — what of him?" the girl asked.

"Dead. Out there where you saw him," I told her and signed to Long Bear, and they ran out and seized hold of his forepaws and drew him in close to the moose. He was as heavy as a full-grown man.

"You are a great hunter," Long Bear signed to me. "You must have a powerful medicine. You shoot a seizer right in the center of his breast, you turn and put an arrow straight into the heart of a moose. Truly, the sun loves you. I plainly see your personality: you will rise up, and up, and become a great chief. You will have a name that will be feared by all the enemy tribes of the plains and mountains."

"Almost-brother, as our friend thinks of you, so do I," Dove Woman told me.

"I wish that you would not praise me so much. I do not deserve it, and, besides, it may make me unlucky. Come. We waste time!" I answered them, and laid down my bow and arrows and began sharpening my knife with a smooth piece of rock.

The Dreadful River Cave

"I cannot help you skin your kills, but I can bring up the horses. I go now for them," Long Bear signed us.

"No. Don't you do it, you with your bad arm and no weapons. You sit down and rest, and as soon as we have butchered the moose I shall go for the horses while almost-brother skins his seizer," Dove Woman told him.

Long Bear did not make any answer to that. He walked slowly away from us along the trail that the game had made in the willows, and sat down at the outer edge of them. We turned to the moose, swung his head around to prop his great body belly up, and went to work. Fat the thickness of two fingers showed as I cut the skin down along the point of the brisket, and Dove Woman laughed happily when she saw it.

"Oh, how glad our old people will be when they see us unload this rich meat!" she told me.

"Yes, and the children, too. How the little ones will dance around it!" I answered.

We had the big animal skinned, and the meat about half cut up, when we missed Long Bear. Dove Woman ran out to where he had been sitting, then clear around the belt of willows, calling him, and back to me.

"Almost-brother, he has gone!" she cried. "Gone after the horses, no doubt, and I told him not to! He should have minded me! I fear for his safety; he so helpless with his not-yet-healed arm!"

Again the Enemy

"Oh, well, don't worry about him. He will be careful of his broken arm, and the horses are very gentle; he can easily lead them with his sound arm and hand," I answered.

We finished cutting up the moose meat, with strips of skin tying the big pieces and the ribs in sets of two so that they would balance evenly when loaded upon the horses, and then we skinned the big seizer very carefully, head and tail and claws and all, and I was so happy over my success in obtaining the hide that, when I made the last cut and freed it from the carcass, I took it up and danced with it.

"At last I am to have what I have long wanted, a fine saddle robe," I told my helper.

"Yes. And I shall tan it for you. I shall make it as soft as the wings of a butterfly, and its skin side as white as the snow up there upon the mountain-top!" she exclaimed.

"When you were born and Old Sun named you, he made a mistake; he should have named you Generous Woman. Always you are working for others, doing nothing for yourself."

"Ha! To help others, that is happiness," she said.

And was she not right? One may not neglect his own family, but over and above their needs, to give to the sick, the poor, to help the unfortunate, that, my son, makes for true happiness.

We went out to the edge of the willows and sat

The Dreadful River Cave

down and waited for Long Bear to appear with the horses. He had been gone long enough, we thought, to have been twice to the point of the lake and back. But still we waited, and became uneasy about him, and more uneasy, and at last I slung my bow and arrow case upon my back and took up my gun, and Dove Woman shouldered her gun, and we set out upon his trail. He broke from the timber just as we were about to enter it, and behind him were no horses. He was walking very fast; his painted face was all streaked with perspiration. He saw us and threw up his sound arm and signed: "The horses are gone!"

"We were careless. We did not securely fasten their ropes. They are back-trailing to camp," I signed.

"Not so," he answered. "They have been stolen. The thief was in such a hurry that he did not untie one of the ropes: he cut it where you had knotted it around a little tree."

Did our hearts sink as we watched him sign that to us? They surely did! Dove Woman cried: "Oh, he must be mistaken! They can't be stolen!" But she knew that they had been taken from us, the cut rope was proof enough of that, and she went suddenly weak and sat down in the grass. And I — I had a gone feeling in my stomach at the thought of what the loss of the horses would mean to us. To begin with, here were four big pack-loads of moose meat that would become flyblown and sour before

Again the Enemy

to-morrow's sun.[1] And without horses it would be impossible for Dove Woman and me to keep our camp of twenty-two people supplied with meat. I just had to recover those horses, or somehow get two in place of them or we should starve. Remember that we left our dogs, many of them big, powerful animals that could carry a pack and drag a travois, with our relatives. We dared not have them with us, for their barking would attract enemies straight to our camp.

"Almost-brother, what, oh, what are we to do?" Dove Woman asked me brokenly through her tears.

"Take to our hungry ones all the moose meat that we can carry. When we get to camp we will council together," I told her and signed to Long Bear, and led them back to the willows.

We loaded ourselves, Dove Woman and I, with clear meat. I could not leave there my fine seizer's skin, so threw it over Long Bear's shoulder for him to carry. He wanted also to pack some meat, but we would not let him do that; he had to protect his healing arm. It was with sad hearts that we left the little belt of willows, where, so short a time back, we had been so happy over our great pile of fat meat, and my killing, too, of the big seizer. We hurried along our back trail to the place where we had left the horses, and laid aside our packs and looked about for signs of the enemy. As Long Bear had told us, we found that one of the ropes had been

[1] An adult bull moose weighed from 1200 to 1400 pounds.

187

The Dreadful River Cave

cut: Dove Woman's rope it was. After passing it around the little tree she had tied many knots in it, and the stealer had thought that he had n't the time to undo them. Right then I suspected that it was a lone enemy who had taken the horses. Had there been more, not only would they have been in no hurry to get away with the animals; they would have lain in wait for us and sent our shadows to the Sand Hills. Look as we would we could find not one track of the enemy; but there were tracks of the horses; they had been taken from the place on the full jump. We took up our loads of meat and followed their trail. It led us down along the lake, and across the outlet, and on down the slope of the great red mountain, and there at the end of it, and just above the falls, we found that the enemy had turned them into the across-the-mountains trail and taken them up it.

"Ha! Just as I thought: some West-Side enemy has them!" Dove Woman exclaimed.

I said nothing. I was too low-hearted to talk, and angry, also, because I could not make up my mind what would now be best for us to do. I was very anxious to council with my father and Old Sun. I led on down the valley, leaving the trail and making straight for camp, and we arrived there and threw down our loads while the sun was still high above the mountains.

CHAPTER XII

I SEEK MY OWN

OUR people had seen us coming, and were gathered in front of my father's lodge, silently, fearfully watching our approach. My mother was the first to speak: "Oh, my son! What misfortune is upon us now — where are your horses?" she asked me.

"Gone! Gone on the trail to the West! They were stolen from us while we hunted," I answered.

"But you made a killing. You bring meat; good, fat moose meat, if I mistake not!" cried old Red Wing Woman, bending over the load that I had thrown down.

"Oh, yes!" Dove Woman put in. "It is moose meat. First he killed a big seizer — see its skin there across Long Bear's shoulder. And then he killed a very big, fat bull moose. We butchered it; prepared the meat for packing while Long Bear went for the horses. He came back to us without them; they had been stolen by some West-Side enemy. Oh, it is heart-sickening, our bad luck! That great pile of fat meat to spoil there, we to go half-hungry here!" And with that she sat down and covered her head with her robe and cried. And that frightened the little children and they began to

The Dreadful River Cave

cry; and their mothers to all talk at once, soothing them, and bewailing the loss of the horses.

"Oh, come! Come with us away from these disturbers of our quiet. Let us hear all about it," my father told me, and led the way to Old Sun's lodge, Long Bear going with us. We took seats within, and while Old Sun filled a pipe and started it going, I told all the happenings of the day. It did not take me long.

"Well, well!" my father exclaimed when I had finished. "This is hard luck for us, but especially for you and your almost-sister, my son. You two are our food providers — you will now have to hunt constantly and pack in upon your backs what is necessary to keep life in our bodies. But you shall have help. Some of our younger women shall follow you and pack in what they can carry of your kills!"

"Ai! That they shall do! My youngest woman, Arrow Woman, is very strong; she can carry enough meat to keep this lodge supplied," said Old Sun.

"Well, listen to me," I told them. "I shall not make a pack-horse of myself, nor do I intend that my mother or almost-mothers shall kill themselves with hard work. I start right now for the West-Side. I shall bring back my horses or two enemy horses in place of them."

"But you have no thought for us; without you we must starve!" cried Old Sun.

"No, you will not starve. I have thought it all

I Seek My Own

out," I replied. "There is the big pile of moose meat. Long Bear and Dove Woman and your young women and my almost-mothers can cut it into sheets and dry it right where it is, and then easily pack it here. And if it does not last until I return, then Dove Woman can kill more meat."

"Son, absolutely I approve your plan!" my father exclaimed. "And don't you worry about us. True, I am old and weak, and my eyes are dim, but go your way; bring back your horses or enemy horses, and enemy scalps if you can possibly take them, and have no thought for us. I, Bear Eagle, am not so far gone but what, in this time of great need, I can again pull trigger, and — whoom! drop a buffalo in his tracks!"

"I am glad to hear you say that. I shall leave at once for the West," I said.

"No. Not until we have made medicine for you. We were going to do that anyhow, but now there is still greater need that we pray and make sacrifices for you!" my father exclaimed, and shouted to my mother to come to us.

"Hurry, you and your sisters, and put up a sweat lodge for us. We have to pray for our son: he soon starts on the trail of his horses," he told her when she appeared in the doorway.

My mother was a wise woman, a brave woman; she saw the great need that we had for those horses and said not one word against my purpose to recover them. She smiled at me encouragingly and

191

The Dreadful River Cave

hurried away to get help to prepare the lodge and heat the rocks. I went home to collect the few things that I was to take with me. Long Bear followed, and I told him and Dove Woman what I had decided to do. He wanted to go with me, begged to go, but I would not listen to his pleading: "Crippled as you are, you would only make my undertaking more dangerous to me. You can do more good by remaining here and helping the women," I told him.

The willow-framed, leather-covered sweat lodge was soon ready for us, and my father, Old Sun, and I crawled into it, the women passed in the red-hot rocks, and my father sprinkled them with water and prayed for my success and safety in my trailing of the stolen horses. Old Sun did the same, calling, too, upon his medicine to protect me. And I prayed. And soon we went out and bathed and put on our clothing, and I felt strong in body and strong in mind for my venture. I hung on a tree a fine belt as a sacrifice to the sun.

My mother called to us to come and eat. The broiled moose meat tasted good. I finished eating, and slung my war sack upon my back, along with my bow-case. In the sack were several pairs of moccasins, an awl, sinew thread, needle, paint, and a good quantity of pemmican which my careful mother had been keeping against a time of need. Lastly I slung on my powder-horn and ball-pouch and took up my gun.

I Seek My Own

"I go," I said.

"Yes, go," they all told me, and I left them. They did not say to me, as you white people say to one another, "Good-bye!" What an unlucky word that is. It means, I take it, that the person you so address will never return.

The sun was now low in the west. I hurried down the slope and struck the big trail near the falls. Their roaring seemed to call me. I sneaked down to our hiding-place behind the junipers and looked through them. A lone otter was sitting upon the rock at the foot of the big pool, eating a trout; proof enough that the Under-Water person was away back in his dreadful cave. "Your time is coming; it is not far off!" I called out to him, but of course he did not hear me; the roar of the water was ever in his ears. I sneaked back to the trail and hurried up it.

When night came I was well up the valley behind the big, red-rock mountain. For some distance back the tracks of my horses in the trail had showed me that the stealer or stealers of them had been in no hurry; nowhere had they been urged to a pace faster than a walk. I felt that by pressing on all through the night, and with but short rests during the following day I could overtake the outfit before they arrived at the foot of the far slope of the mountains. Nor did the darkness impede my progress. I had no difficulty in keeping upon the broad and well-worn trail.

The Dreadful River Cave

When the moon came up, some time before midnight, I was nearing a small pond, and beyond it could see the last steep slope leading up to the top of this backbone-of-the-world. As I came to the pond I thought that I caught a faint odor of smoke; believed myself mistaken, then smelled it again. I turned off the trail at that, upon the side away from the lake, and went on very slowly and cautiously, and soon came to a small fireplace covered with white, fluffy ashes. I put my hand down into them and felt heat, and was glad; here the enemy had rested for a time, and by the length of that time I was just that much nearer to him. And then, a step or two away from the fireplace, I discovered a side of roasted ribs but half-eaten; the feaster's eyes had been larger than his hunger. I cut off and threw away the ribs that he had stripped, and went on my way eating the portion that he had not touched. It was good meat; fat, bighorn meat. I ate it all and by so much saved the pemmican that I was carrying.

Looking ahead, it did not seem far from the little lake to the summit of the range; or perhaps the moonlight deceived me as to the distance; anyhow, I climbed steadily on all through the rest of the night and did not arrive at the summit until day was breaking. The last part of the ascent was across a very steep bed of slide rock resting upon the edge of a cliff of great height. I could not see how far down it dropped; night and a gray, drift-

I Seek My Own

ing, twisting cloud of fog hid the foot of it from me. But from the thin, knife-like edge of the summit of the mountain, close above me, a big rock broke loose and went bounding down the slope, and it was a long time before its crash upon the bottom of the cañon came to my ears. The thought of what would happen to me if I made a misstep gave me a weak feeling in my stomach. I was not used to walking along such terrifying, straight-down-dropping edges of the world. I did the worst thing that I could possibly have done: ran all the rest of the way across that slide. Ran swiftly, blindly on and on, loosening quantities of rock from the edge of the trail that went tinkling down the steep and off over the edge of the cliff. Nothing but the sure favor of the gods kept me from going off it with the slides. I passed the dangerous place, and a narrow gap in the crest of the mountain, and looked off upon a country new to me, a country whose aspect made me shiver.

Here were no sunlit, smiling plains and slender buttes. As far as I could see in any direction there stretched out before me narrow valleys and steep ranges of mountains, covered, all of them — yes, the very tops of the mountains — with dark, heavy timber. Not even one little grassy prairie was there to brighten that heart-depressing outlook. As I stared off at it I did not wonder that the West-Side tribes were always, and at the risk of their lives, sneaking out from the dim shade of their endless

The Dreadful River Cave

forest to hunt upon our sunny plains. Oh, what a terrible country was theirs! Again I shivered. I hated to go down into it!

But go I must. Again I took the trail, zigzagging down over brushy ledges for a little way, and then entering the dark timber. The tracks of my two horses in it were so fresh that it seemed they could not be far ahead of me. Even here on the down slope the enemy had allowed them to walk. I went on· at a swifter pace than that and never slowed up until I arrived at the foot of the mountain and the edge of a large stream of clear, swift-flowing water. There I sat down and drank thirstily, and opened my sack and ate some of my good mother's pemmican. I was now very tired and sleepy, but would not give way to my feelings. The enemy was close ahead of me; if I did not now press on and overtake him, I should never see my horses until I found them in the herds of the camp for which he was heading, and that might be a long way down in that gloomy country of the West. I drank again at the river's edge and went on.

And now I perceived that here my horses had been urged into a trot, and, a little way farther on, into a steady lope which was never broken except at sharp bends of the trail or where a fallen log, too high to be jumped, obstructed it. I began to lose hope of overtaking them, but still I ran on and on, thinking that, perhaps, after a time of this swift traveling, the enemy would be satisfied with the

I Seek My Own

distance he had come and make camp. He, too,
needed sleep and rest, but not so much as I did. He
had ridden all that long way while I had walked
and run, and carried no little load of weapons and
war sack. Toward the last of that hot and windless
morning I just staggered along the trail and my
mind seemed to become clouded. Finally, when the
sun was almost straight over my head, I stumbled
against a tree-root sticking up in the trail and fell,
and was so completely tired that I could not get
up. I crawled into some thick willows to the left of
the trail and bordering the river, and without re-
moving my bow-case and the pack from my back,
stretched out upon my side and fell asleep.

I did not awake until long after dark, and, oh,
how angry I was because I had slept so long! Gone,
surely gone, was all chance of my overtaking my
enemy and my horses before he could arrive at the
camp of his people, wherever it was. I sat up and
removed the things from my back. With many a
groan I got upon my feet, all swollen, and my legs
so stiff that I could hardly walk. I staggered through
the brush and out upon a sandy shore of the river;
took off my clothes and rolled into the water and
remained in it a long time, rubbing my feet and
legs and taking the soreness out of them. Then I
dressed and returned to my resting-place, ate sparingly of my pemmican, and again lay down. As I
could not overtake my enemy, I had decided to
follow him at a leisurely pace. I was crazy to have

197

The Dreadful River Cave

followed him so recklessly. Had he turned off the trail and lain in wait for me, he would now be taking my scalp as well as my horses to count *coup* upon before his people. Why had n't he done that? Either because he had no thought that he would be pursued or that he was a coward.

When I awoke again day had come. Something was wrong. At first I could not think what it was, and then I knew: it was the awful silence about me. Over in our country a hundred varieties of little birds awoke us with their happy singing and chirping, calling to us that day was coming, and then the sun reddened the tops of our lodges and we opened our eyes and saw the bright, sacred color and were glad. But here! Not a single bird call broke the silence of the gloomy forest! True, the river was not silent, but its voice was sad enough; a deep, hoarse rising and falling roar that was more oppressive than the silence of the forest. Feeling very poor, indeed, I took up my belongings and went out to the river, had another bath, and ate some more of my pemmican. But little of it remained; only enough for two or three more meals, surely not sufficient for my need while in this enemy country. I determined to kill some meat and roast a quantity of it to carry with me.

I had seen some deer tracks the previous evening, and now as I went on they became more plentiful, and occasionally I caught sight of the waving white tail of a deer as it fled from my approach. I

I Seek My Own

had not gone far, however, when I saw a fine buck out at the edge of the river, and thought that he might come toward me when he finished drinking. I set my gun up against a tree, and with an arrow fitted to my bow stood ready for him. He did come toward me. I stood motionless behind a tree, and when he was about to cross the trail I shot my arrow deep into his side, and he turned and ran straight from me and fell and died right in the trail. I hurried to him, recovered my arrow, and dragged him well into the brush to the right, and then brushed out all signs of my work. He was quite fat. I cut out his tongue, a side of ribs and the loin meat, and carried them across the narrow valley to the foot of the mountain-slope. Here was plenty of wood for my purpose; dry and fallen quaking aspen and birch. In my bow-case was a fire-drill, in my war sack a fire-board. I got them out, heaped the board with finely shredded birch-bark, made a turn around the drill with my bow-cord and twirled it into the board, and the heat that it made soon set the bark afire. I transferred the bark to a small pile of the dry wood that I had previously gathered and it began to burn — as I knew it would — with so little smoke that none was visible above the tops of the surrounding trees. I set my portions of meat up before the fire and thoroughly roasted them, ate the tongue, stuffed the rest into my war sack, and went on down the valley.

The Dreadful River Cave

I thought of all that I had heard our warriors tell about this West-Side country. As I remembered their descriptions of it, all the streams running westward along here soon united and formed a river that ran into a very large lake,[1] and the lake was only three or four days' travel from the Two Medicine Pass over which I had come. There were large prairies bordering the lake, and there the Kalispels generally camped and grazed their large bands of horses. I believed that my enemy was a Kalispel and was heading for that prairie-bordered lake. If so, in three days, at the most, I would sight the big camp of his people and their herds of horses.

In the afternoon of this day I came to the place where my enemy had made camp and rested after his long ride across the mountains, and now, seeing the tracks in the shore of the river, and the signs around the dead fireplace, I made absolutely sure that he was alone. I found where he had picketed out my horses to graze; they had not eaten very much of the grasses and vines that they could reach. There was not much ash in the little fireplace. My enemy had taken but a short rest there, and was now, I believed, more than a day of foot-traveling ahead of me.

Late in this afternoon I came to where the trail crossed the stream, and so I crossed over to the south side of it. The valley had been widening

[1] Flathead Lake.

I Seek My Own

steadily, and now, close ahead, it merged into a still wider valley coming in from the northeast, and in this valley was a real river, swift and deep and of clear but greenish color. This was, as I knew from what I had heard, the big river running into the prairie-bordered lake of the Kalispels. I made camp at the point where the stream that I had been following ran into it.

On the following morning I was on my way before daylight, and in the middle of the forenoon found myself at the end of the big valley and at the outer edge of the mountains, rising steeply to the north and south as far as I could see. Before me was a rather flat and heavily timbered country, and across it, faint and blue and many days' travel to the west, was another range of mountains. I had heard of them, too; they were the mountains of the River People,[1] and beyond them was a very large lake, along which the River People lived, except when they were sneaking out to the edge of our plains to steal our buffaloes and other game, and sometimes to raid our horse herds, and perhaps waylay and kill two or three straggling hunters from our camp. They were a foolish people; always they paid dearly for what they did to us, and they knew that they would, yet they could not resist the temptation to come out again and again upon our rich and endless plains.

[1] The Pend d'Oreille tribe of Indians, living upon the shores of the lake of that name.

The Dreadful River Cave

The trail now ran close beside the big river, flowing to the southwest, and following it I several times during the day crossed fair-sized streams putting into the river from the east. The first one of these, I was sure, had its source in the pass at the head of the South Fork of our Two Medicine River, for there was a well-worn trail beside it that, some days back, had been all cut up by a large camp of people moving west. I believed that they were the enemy that I had frightened away from the Two Medicine Valley, after killing their medicine man.

I laughed when I thought how they had stampeded for their country, believing that the warriors of a whole tribe of Blackfeet would soon be after them. Had they known the truth, how quickly they would have wiped out our little camp of nahwak'-o-sis-growers!

Near sundown of this day I came to another, a fourth stream, putting into the big river from the east, and beside it a trail larger and more deeply worn than the big trail that I was following, and into which it merged. There were no fresh tracks of any foot- or horse-travelers in this trail. I stood looking at it, thinking again of what I had heard about these West-Side trails, and decided that this one was the great trail that came over the mountains at the head of our Point-of-Rocks River,[1] and followed its course down to its junction with Big

[1] Sun River.

I Seek My Own

River,[1] at a point just above the upper one of the Great Falls. It was this trail that the West-Side tribes mostly followed when they came over to steal our game, but they seldom used it at this time of year. They waited until winter was near, then sent scouts ahead to learn if any of our tribes were camping on the upper stretches of Big River and its tributaries. We seldom did winter there, and, finding the country clear, they would come over and remain until spring, hunting, sometimes, along the edge of the mountains southward almost to the country of the Crows. More than once early spring war parties of our tribes had caught them in that part of our country and had killed many of their warriors and taken great numbers of their horses.

Looking back now at the mountains, black and forbidding even in the light of the lowering sun, I measured the distance that I had come from them and believed that I could not be much more than another day's travel from the big lake. I determined to proceed more cautiously, lest I be discovered by wandering hunters from the camp of the Kalispels. There was here but little underbrush in the timber, so I kept to one side of the trail, but close enough constantly to see it and follow its course. When night fell I went out to the river and drank, and ate some of my roast meat, then came

[1] Missouri River. The "country of the Crows" lay to the south of the Yellowstone River.

The Dreadful River Cave

back close to the trail and prepared for a long sleep.
I prayed to the gods for my people and for myself,
and lay down, and just as I was falling asleep I
heard, off to the east, footsteps upon the trail. They
came nearer and I knew what they were: the soft,
quick thudding of many moccasined feet upon the
hard-packed ground. I had no fear for myself,
knowing that I could not possibly be seen, but, oh
how I wanted to see the travelers and know who
they were, whether Kalispels or a war party from
the plains. They might be Crows, or Sioux, or Assiniboines, or, possibly, a party from one of our
Blackfeet tribes.

The gods were good to me. I cannot doubt but
they caused one of the party, just as they were
passing me, to stub his toes against an obstruction
in the trail. "Hau! I have almost broken my toes!
Curse the darkness of this forest!" he cried out in
his pain, and, oh, how pleasant in my ears were
those Blackfeet words.

"My relatives! Whither go you?" I called to
them, and they stopped short, and one asked me:
"You, out there in the darkness, who are you?"

Ha! Well I knew that voice! It was the voice of
Yellow Wolf, chief of our Raven Carriers Society.
I sprang up with my weapons and war sack and
answered as I ran to the trail, "I am your young
friend, Black Elk! Oh, how glad I am that you are
here!

"Ha! He is Black Elk!" the chief exclaimed; and

I Seek My Own

as I came into the trail I was surrounded by a crowd of warriors, embracing me, asking me questions, all talking at once.

"Burners of my ears, be quiet, all of you! allow me to hear myself talk with Black Elk! Sit down, and listen to us, and you will know all," Yellow Wolf commanded, and down we all sat along the sides of the trail.

Now, what do you think was the first question the chief asked me? Why was I there in that West-Side forest?

No. What he said was: "How about the nah-wak'-o-sis? Did you make a large planting of it — and is it growing well?"

I answered that we had more than ten hundred strong-leaved, fast-growing plants of it, and at that they all clapped their hands and cried out how pleased they were. What fine medicine work we were doing, not only for ourselves but for our tribe as well!

Said Yellow Wolf, then, "Go on, Black Elk, relate to us all that has happened to you and your three-lodge camp since you left us."

I did as he asked, excepting that I made no mention of the Under-Water person. I wanted him all to myself. And when I had done, and had been accorded much praise, Yellow Wolf said to me:

"We are seventy men, going to raid the Kalispels. Don't you worry about your two horses; just

205

The Dreadful River Cave

come along with us and you shall have them or enemy horses in their place."

"I am tired out; I have been traveling since before daylight. I can go no farther this night," I answered.

"Ha! Then we shall rest right here with you," he kindly told me, and we all scattered out, seeking soft places upon which to lie and were soon asleep. Myself, I was so sleepy that I could not at that time ask about the doings of the tribe since we had left it.

CHAPTER XIII

GREAT ADVENTURE

O N the following morning, at daybreak, we all
went to the river and bathed, and then, when
we had dressed and were eating sparingly of the
food that we carried, my friends gave me news of
our people. They were encamped at the mouth of
Point-of-Rocks River, from which in all directions
the plains were black with buffaloes. My relatives
were all well. War parties had gone against the
Assiniboines, Crows, and Snakes, and all had returned with many scalps and horses of the enemy.
A youth named Otter Head, while swimming in
Big River, had been seized by the Under-Water
People. He had struggled hard against them, calling piteously for help, but his playmates had not
dared go out to assist him and he had been drawn
down into the depths, never to be seen again.

I shivered when I heard that; it made me realize what danger I must face in fulfillment of my
vow. I wanted, oh, how I wanted to tell these, my
friends, about the dweller in the dreadful river-cave,
and about my vow, and ask their advice. But if
I did that Yellow Wolf would probably say that I
was too young, too inexperienced to face the danger in that black hole in the cliff; that he and the

The Dreadful River Cave

members of his Raven Carriers Society would take upon themselves the vow that I had made. I held my peace.

Yellow Wolf now gave out his orders for the day. We were, he said, a long day's walk from the lake of the Kalispels, where we should likely find all or a part of the tribe encamped. We would keep off the trail and push on as rapidly as possible. He told off four men to precede us as scouts, and after they had been gone some little time, we shouldered our packs and our weapons and followed them.

All that morning and until late in the afternoon our course was through an unbroken and almost level forest. Its gloom, its silence did not now oppress me, for I was in good company. We saw but little signs of game; only a few tracks of whitetail deer. I became more and more convinced that Old Man, after he had made that great forest country, was so much disappointed with his work that he gave it to the meanest of the peoples he had made, the Kalispels, the River People, and the different tribes of the Snake Nation.

It was near sundown when we came upon our scouts, waiting for us. They reported small prairies ahead, and a number of hunting trails, in some of which were fresh horse-tracks.

"Yes, I thought that we were near the first of the prairies," said Yellow Wolf. "Let us now have a short talk and decide upon just what we shall do." He sat down, called to his servant — a youth learning the ways of war — to prepare a pipe for him, and we all seated ourselves around him. Nearly all the members of the party had been in this country raiding its various tribes, not once but many times; the Raven Carriers were all warriors of long experience. But they all had the utmost faith in their leader; because of his bravery, his wise caution, and his sun power — he was a medicine man as well as a chief — he was the chosen head of their Society. And so, when he now called upon them to give their views as to the course to be pursued, they one by one declared that they were more than glad to leave the matter entirely to him.

"So be it!" he exclaimed, and lighted his pipe with fire from the little blaze that the servant had started in front of him, blew smoke to the four world directions, and earnestly prayed the gods to give him wisdom to make his plan, and to bring us all safely through the dangers that we were to meet, and back to our people with plenty of enemy scalps and enemy property. He then passed the pipe, and while we in turn took a whiff of smoke from it, and offered up a short prayer, he sat with head bowed, thinking deeply. At last the pipe, smoked out, came back to his hand. He knocked the ashes out of it, handed it to his servant to put away, and said to us:

"Fresh tracks in the trails hereabout prove that the enemy are camped where I thought that they

The Dreadful River Cave

would be, at the head of the big lake. We are not far from it. We will rest here until some time after dark, and then I shall lead you. I know this country so well that almost I could go through it with my eyes shut. Before midnight we shall see the camp of the enemy, and when we do, I shall plan our attack upon it. Now, when I say to you that you must rest, I mean just that. I want you all to sleep, for only by doing that can one really freshen and strengthen his body and mind, and before this night is over you will need all the strength and courage that you can obtain. I, myself, shall not sleep. I go out here a little way to make medicine for our safety and success in our undertaking against the enemy this night."

Solemn words those were. After hearing them we none of us felt like talking. We lay down well away from one another, and if the others did as I did, they put their minds upon the battle that was soon to take place and prayed the gods again and again for help before they fell asleep.

It was early night when Yellow Wolf awakened us. We went to the river, where we drank, and ate some of our food, and were then strong to follow our chief.

"We will take no chances," he told us. "Enemy scouts may be watching the trails, so we will keep well off from them. Come! We start!"

As we advanced, the little prairie openings in the forest became more numerous, but we crossed

Great Adventure

none of them and kept always in the timber. Our course was therefore like that of a river, bending over to the right and to the left down its valley. I walked next to young Elk Ribs, Yellow Wolf's servant, and after a time he began to complain: "I don't like this," he said to me. "We are traveling this way and that way, making a snakelike trail. We should go straight toward that which we seek, and so save valuable time."

Ha! Yellow Wolf happened to hear what he said, and turned upon him: "Oh, wise one," he said to him, "I am sorry that my judgment of the proper course to take through this forest does not seem right to you. You started out with us as my servant, but already you have become a wise old warrior. Take you my place. Lead on; we follow you!"

And at that some of us laughed. But others became angry and called out to Yellow Wolf to make the boy take the back trail for home, lest he cause us bad luck.

"No, my friends," he answered them. "Remember that Elk Ribs is only a boy. He spoke thoughtlessly, heedlessly, as boys will do. He is a good servant. I need him. I know that he will not bring us bad luck. Come, we proceed."

"Oh, great chief! I don't know why I said what I did. You are good to me; you pity me. Gladly will I die for you," Elk Ribs told him, and cried a little as we started on. I patted his back and told him to cheer up; that all was well.

The Dreadful River Cave

On and on we went through the dark forest. As well as we could through the tops of the trees we kept watch upon the Seven Persons, swinging around in the northern sky. At last they told us that it was midnight, and Yellow Wolf, bringing us to a halt and pointing up to them, said: "You see where they stand. Night-Light will soon appear. When we see her rising we shall be very close to the big lake, and — I hope — our enemy and their big bands of horses."

It was not long after that when the night began to lighten, and then, just as Night-Light appeared in the east, we heard, faint but unmistakable, the long, shrill cry of a loon. It was pleasant in our ears; it told us that we were near the big lake; that we should soon see it. And presently we did. Arriving at the edge of a long, wide prairie, we looked down across it and saw wind-ruffled water stretching away to the south and west until it was lost in the night. We could see no horses upon the prairie nor camp of the enemy, but while we stood there staring out at it, somewhere off ahead a lone wolf howled, and then, at the upper end of the prairie there broke out the angry barking and howling of dogs.

"Ha! Off there is the enemy camp!" some one exclaimed.

"Yes, there it is, in the edge of the timber bordering the river, and just where I believed it would be," said Yellow Wolf.

Great Adventure

"Apparently a camp without horses; a war party has been here ahead of us and gotten away with them," young Elk Ribs whimpered.

Truly, his thought was also mine. I suddenly felt low-hearted. I had come this long way after my horses and was not to recover them. But the others who heard the boy laughed softly, and Yellow Wolf exclaimed:

"Well, they have made our work difficult for us. They are expecting a raid upon their horses and have corralled them in the timber, and doubtless placed a guard around them. Come, the night is more than half gone; follow me and we shall see what we can do."

Keeping well within the edge of the timber, we headed the prairie and turned down along the river toward the lake, and then Yellow Wolf halted us and said that we were to remain right where we were while he went on for a look at the camp. He disappeared in the dark shadows of the timber. Again a wolf howled, and when the camp dogs answered him we became quite excited: we were no more than a hundred steps from the edge of the camp. We carefully examined our weapons and anxiously awaited the return of our chief.

He could not have been gone long when he came sneaking back, but to us it seemed that it had been a whole moon of time. We crowded close around him and he said to us: "Well, it is as I thought: the point of timber is one big corral full of horses.

The Dreadful River Cave

The fence runs from the river-bank out to the prairie at a point just below the camp, and from there down along the edge of the timber and out a little way into the lake. Near the river I sneaked inside the fence, and keeping well back among the horses, and walking very slowly, followed it around nearly to the lake. There are watchers here and there along it. I saw the red glow of one's pipe, and heard two others talking. I saw and counted forty lodges; there may be a few more than that — "

"Ha!" a big warrior, named One Horn, exclaimed. "Let us say that there are fifty lodges and two fighting men to a lodge. A hundred men, and we are seventy. Come! Let us attack that camp! We are Blackfeet! Good for three or four times our number of these West-Side forest-dwellers!"

"One Horn, my friend, you talk foolishly," Yellow Wolf told him. "I did not lead you all here needlessly to risk your lives nor mine. Dead, we are of no use to our tribe and our families; our shadows cannot fight their battles nor provide them with food. We are here to injure the enemy as much as we can with least possible risk to us. Hear me. This will we do: go back up the river a little way and find a good place in which to hide, and then, while you all remain there, I shall come out and find a place from which to watch this camp and its horse herds during the day, and thus learn just what is best for us to do."

"Oh, you must have your way about it, you are

our chief," One Horn told him, "but for once I should like to have my way. My whole body aches to get at the enemy and wipe some of them out."

We had none of us spoken a word during this argument, and by our silence One Horn well knew that he was alone in his desire to make an immediate attack upon the enemy. No matter what he had proposed to do he would have had no followers, for he had twice led a war party, and each time his crazy bravery, his lack of foresight, had caused the death of more than half of his followers.

Well, we followed Yellow Wolf up the river for quite a long way, and after some search in the darkness under the great trees at last found a good hiding-place in a heavy growth of willows about fifty steps back from a cutbank of the river. There our chief left us. We slept until daylight, then went to a sloping shore above the cutbank and drank and bathed, and hurried back into the willows. We ate some of our food, for many of us the last that we had, and then stretched out upon the ground for a long day of rest. We all soon became very sleepy, and One Horn finally sat up and said: "This will not do; one or two of us must be constantly on watch, lest some of the enemy, wandering this way, discover us and bring the whole camp of warriors to surprise us. I will take first watch. Who will sit up with me?"

"I will," I answered, before any one else could offer, and moved out with him to the lower edge

The Dreadful River Cave

of the willows. From there we could see a part of the prairie. Between us and the river were a few large cottonwood trees, but we could not see the water because of the high cutbank.

We had not sat there very long when we saw band after band of horses moving slowly out upon the prairie as they grazed, and with each band rode a herder, ready at the first sign of anything suspicious to turn his animals back with a rush to the corral behind the camp.

"It is just as I thought it would be," One Horn told me. "We shall not be able to raid the herds out there. We have, some of us, to attack the camp while the others break an opening in the corral and drive out the horses. Without doubt our chief will allow me to lead the attack. I am glad. Oh, sun, hurry! Hurry across the blue to your far-away lodge in the West! Oh, night, come quickly and hide our advance upon this camp of our enemy!"

By twos and threes and more, hunters were now riding out across the prairie and entering the forest upon their daily quest for meat. Judging from the signs of game that we had seen, I said to One Horn that I thought they often went hungry to bed.

"No, not exactly hungry," he answered. "Their women gather large quantities of many different kinds of roots, and they all fill their stomachs with them when meat is scarce. Ha! Think of it! Depending upon tasteless, woodlike roots for one's daily food!"

Great Adventure

"Yes. That must be a sort of living death," I agreed.

As the morning wore on we became very sleepy and with difficulty kept our eyes open. But we saw nothing, heard nothing of the enemy but the far-off herders until noon, when we discovered a lone woman running toward us from the direction of the camp. She came swiftly up through the timber, pausing now and then to look back, and presently we saw her pursuer, a lone man coming fast upon her trail. She came straight toward us and stopped and hesitated when about twenty or thirty steps from our hiding-place. I thought her the most beautiful girl — with the exception of Dove Woman — that I had ever seen. She was tall and slender, long-haired, big-eyed, and, oh, what terrible fear those eyes expressed. She looked back and saw that the man was surely gaining upon her, would surely overtake her, and then she turned and looked in our direction, and then toward the river. I became tremendously excited. I wanted to spring up and run to her assistance. One Horn seemed to know what I was thinking; he put out a hand and, pressing my knee, whispered: "Do not move until I tell you to!"

Again the girl looked back at the man, now come quite close, and then with a low, wailing cry she turned and ran straight toward the river. At that I attempted to follow her, but One Horn's heavy hand restrained me: "Not yet! Not yet!" he whis-

The Dreadful River Cave

pered, or rather hissed in my ear. And then the girl was at the edge of the cutbank, and sprang from it and we heard her splash into the water. The man had been running his best to head her off. He gave a roar of anger as she disappeared, dropped his leather robe and his bow and arrows, and sprang off the cutbank after her.

We were up and running as he, too, splashed into the water. We arrived at the edge of the cutbank and saw the girl feebly struggling toward the farther shore, and the man swimming powerfully toward her. One Horn was slightly in advance of me; before I could do so, he fired an arrow down at the man and it struck into his left shoulder. With a terrible cry of pain and surprise he flopped over upon his back and saw us, and to this day I can see the fear that was in his wide-open staring eyes and gray face with its sagging mouth. When he gave his affrighted cry the girl looked back, saw him, saw us, and we could hardly believe our ears when we heard her wail: "Oh, my relatives! help me!"

I was already aiming my arrow at the man; that pitiful cry in my own language put added strength into the muscles of my arms. I sped that arrow more swiftly than I had ever sped arrow before, and it struck into the breast of the woman-stealer clear to the feathering; with a hoarse and strangling gasping for breath he threw up his arms and sank. I dropped my bow and sprang from the cutbank, down, down, deep below the surface of the

Great Adventure

water, and quickly came up and swam out after the girl. I heard a splash behind me and knew that One Horn was also swimming out to assist her. Hampered by heavy, soaked, and clinging gown of buckskin, she was about to sink when we reached her side, I on her right and One Horn on her left. He called out to her to put her hands upon our shoulders. She was clear-headed; she did just that, instead of crazily embracing us as we feared she would. She was of but little hindrance to us; we towed her downstream past the high cutbank and helped her out upon a gravelly shore. She sank down upon it and began to cry, and our companions, who had been roused from their sleep by the wild yell of our enemy when we shot him, came crowding around us. One of them, a young warrior named Bull's Head, leaned down and stared into the girl's face, and clapping hand to mouth exclaimed: "How strange! Antelope Woman! My very own cousin!"

With a loud cry the girl sprang up and embraced him, clung to him, entreating him to save her. He patted her shoulder; smoothed the hair back from her forehead; told her that she was safe. And then One Horn said that we were running great risk by standing there in the open and must hurry back into the willows. On our way to them One Horn and I recovered our weapons and robes. We had not brought our guns out of the thicket.

Many of our party had recognized the girl, but I

The Dreadful River Cave

could not remember ever to have seen her before. She was a daughter of a North Blackfeet man, Turtle Back, whose sister was the mother of Bull's Head. We seated ourselves around her in the shelter of the willows and waited for her to tell us how she came to be in this camp of the enemy. She soon ceased crying, and said:

"It is all like a bad dream! Last moon my people were camped north of the Sweetgrass Hills, on Little River. I had just become the wife of Leaning Pine. We had set up a lodge of our own and were, oh, so happy — perhaps some of you knew him?"

"Yes, yes," several of us answered.

"Well, he is dead! They killed him!" she faltered, pointing off toward the camp, and broke down and cried.

"Ha! This night they shall pay for his life!" One Horn exclaimed, and a murmur of assent went around our circle.

The girl recovered her voice after a time, and continued: "My man said that I must have a red-cloth dress and yellow-metal bracelets. He began trapping beavers with which to buy them of the Traders-of-the-North. We went farther and farther from camp up Little River, trapping the beavers and taking their skins, and one day, while we were re-setting the traps, a war party of these Kalispels suddenly burst out of the brush and shot down my man, and I was captured by the one whom you killed out there in the river. He was the chief of the party, so he claimed the two horses that my man and I had been riding, and told his men to go on and take what they could of the Blackfeet herds, and right there he made me his wife! Oh, how I hated him! How I hated him! I tried to kill myself, but he took my knife away from me. I ran and threw myself into the deep water of the river, trying to drown, and he dragged me out of it and laughed at me.

"At midnight his men returned with a number of horses and I was tied upon one, and we rode and rode, seldom resting, until we arrived at this camp. Here, when he was out hunting or with his horses, his mother kept close watch of me. This morning he left the lodge, and when he had been gone some time, his mother lay down and fell asleep. My chance had come. I sneaked from the lodge back into the timber, and started up this way, hoping to escape and return to my people, and then, after a time, I saw that terrible man upon my trail. Well, you know the rest. Oh, I can't tell you how happy I was when I looked back, after he gave that awful yell of pain, and saw that you had shot him! I thought that I should probably drown, but he was to die first. I was glad! Glad!"

"Yes. And now, take courage, little cousin," Bull's Head told her. "We shall protect you. Go you now farther back in the willows and dry your clothes. We are all to you just as though we were your very own brothers."

The Dreadful River Cave

"Ai! Ai! We are that!" we all told her, and she arose and left us.

Later in the day, when she returned to us, dry and with a sad little smile upon her face, we got from her what information we wanted about the camp of the enemy. She thought that it numbered about a hundred and thirty fighting men. They were expecting a raid by warriors from her tribe, and so had built the corral into which the horses were run shortly before sundown and guarded by some of the young men during the night.

I offered the girl the robe of the man that we had killed, but she shivered and would not take it, so I gave her mine and wore the other.

We thought it likely that some of the men of the camp would be sent out by the mother of the dead man to look for him and the girl, but the day passed and we saw none but the distant horse-herders. Night came and Yellow Wolf returned to us, and was not a little surprised to learn what excitement we had had during his absence. He said that his day watch of the enemy had been useless, that he could see but one way for us to get away with a large number of enemy horses, and that was for the many of us to attack the camp while the few were breaking down the corral and driving the animals out.

"Just what I proposed that we should do!" One Horn exclaimed.

"Yes. But I had to try to plan a better way, did

Great Adventure

I not? You all know what risks we take when we attack an enemy camp. If you do not wish to take those risks, speak out and tell me so," said Yellow Wolf.

None answered him. Of course not. Who would — no matter how great his fear — acknowledge that he was an afraid-heart?

CHAPTER XIV

I ENTER THE DREADFUL CAVE

WELL, then, we will divide into two parties; one of fifty, to attack the camp, and the rest to raid the corral. Which ones of you will make up the attacking party?" Yellow Wolf asked.

We all of us, every last one of us, declared that we wanted to be of that party.

"And which of you will go into the corral?"

To that question he got no answer. "Ah! I see! You force me to decide the make-up of that party," he said, and named the men, all of them the youngest and least experienced of us. I was surprised that I was not selected, and swelled all up with pride that I was considered a real warrior.

"Oh, I am glad! I am to be with your party," I told One Horn, standing close beside me.

"Not so! You are to be with neither party," said Yellow Wolf, turning and facing me. "Upon your shoulders rests a burden of the greatest value to our tribe. Your one duty is to protect those growers of the sacred nah-wak'-o-sis, over there on the Two Medicine. We shall get for you the horses that you need, and to-morrow you shall be well upon your way back to your camp. No, my son, you may not risk your life in what we are to do this night, not if we can help it."

I Enter the Dreadful Cave

The whole party voiced their approval of the chief's words. I saw that it would be useless for me to plead to join in the attack, and asked what I was to do.

"You and this poor young widow, you will remain at the edge of the prairie, straight out from here, and wait for us to come to you," he answered, and turned and told all to be sure to remember that it was to be the meeting-place of both parties. That the corral-breakers would arrive there first, and must remain there until joined by the camp-raiders.

There followed a long wait. Night came and we went out to the river, below the cutbank, and drank, and ate the very last of our food. The sacred pipe was filled and lighted, and passed around the circle, and all prayed for success against the enemy, and various sacrifices were promised the sun. We kept watch of the Seven Persons; when they pointed to near midnight, Yellow Wolf arose and called to us to follow him. He led straight out to the edge of the prairie, told me that I should stop right there with the widow, and cautioned the others to mark well this place where they were all to meet us. They left us, and we sat down anxiously to await their return.

The girl was very low-hearted. I did my best to turn her thoughts from the loss of her man and her capture by the enemy, but soon found that she was not even listening to what I said. I ceased talking. I could hear nothing but the occasional low sobbing of the girl, and that finally made me low-hearted. I began to fear all kinds of things: that my little camp over across on the Two Medicine was in trouble; that Yellow Wolf and his warriors would fail in their attack upon the enemy; and, finally, I, myself, was soon to get into terrible danger.

"Oh, sun, and you, my medicine," I prayed, "have pity for us! My relatives — all of our little camp of nah-wak'-o-sis-growers, guard them from all dangers! Grant long life and plenty to all our tribe, and to our brother tribes! And guide me safely back to the Two Medicine that I may kill that dweller in the river cave, and thus fulfill my vow to you!"

I felt better when I had said that prayer. And then, for the first time, the girl spoke to me: "I loved your prayer; it has done me good," she said. "But tell me — who is the 'dweller in the river cave' that you have vowed to kill?"

I made her promise not to tell any of the war party about him, and then she soon knew all; not only about the Under-Water person, but also the adventures of Dove Woman and Long Bear and myself — the whole story of our little camp since we had pitched our lodges upon the Two Medicine Ridge. As I went on with the story I knew by her frequent exclamations that I had at last turned her thoughts from her own troubles.

"Ah! What a fine young woman is that almost-sister of yours!" she said. "Oh, that I could know

I Enter the Dreadful Cave

her! What a comfort she would be to me in this my time of awful grief!"

"Ai! That she would!" I said.

And then we sprang to our feet: away down the river guns were booming; we could even hear the shouting of the warriors; the attack upon the camp had opened. I became so excited that I could not stand still. I wanted to be down there, side by side with my people as they fought our hated enemy. I was even tempted to leave the girl and hurry down there.

She must have known my thoughts: "Oh, my friend," she pleaded, grasping my sleeve, "I know that it is hard for you, but I am sure that you will not disobey the order of your chief!"

"No. Right here we stop until they come to us," I assured her.

The shooting and the shouting lasted for some time, and as it began to die away we heard the far-off thunder of horses' feet. The moon had come up by that time, and presently we saw a great herd of the animals approaching us, and behind them many riders urging them forward with flailing ropes. They rushed by us and called out to the riders: "Head them! Head them! Here we are!" In a very short time we had them rounded up, and my ropes upon two, one for the girl and one for me. I counted the riders; they were twenty. I was glad.

"Well, how was it?" I asked one.

The Dreadful River Cave

"It was too easy," he answered. "We sneaked into the corral and Yellow Wolf gave us plenty of time; we had all caught horses before he and those with him attacked the camp. When the firing began we tore down a part of the corral below the camp and drove out this great band and came away with it, and none of us even saw one of the enemy. Not a gun nor an arrow was fired at us."

All was now quiet below and had been for some time. Several of the riders proposed that they go back to the camp, but the leader, Crow Body, told them no. Yellow Wolf had particularly ordered him to see that the horse-takers remained right here, and here they should stay until the fighters joined them.

And then we saw them coming, and, oh, how anxiously we watched them! And when they had come near, Crow Body cried out: "How many are you?"

"We are all here! All here, none wounded!" Yellow Wolf answered.

What, after all that fighting — not a man of them injured? We could hardly believe our ears.

"Yes. And we have counted *coups*," One Horn roared. "Myself, I have three scalps!"

Others began to count their *coups*.

"Cease that! Out with your ropes and catch horses!" Yellow Wolf cried, and we were soon all mounted. There remained something like three hundred loose animals; we split them up into small

I Enter the Dreadful Cave

bands that we could easily herd along, and struck out upon our homeward trail.

Day had come when we arrived at the fork of the trail that I was to follow, and Yellow Wolf called a halt. "I am minded to send some of my men with you to see you safe to your camp," he told me.

"No. I shall be very cautious. I know that I can make home all right. I just want another horse," I answered.

"Here it is, and I shall ride it," said the young widow.

We all stared at her. "Are you crazy?" her cousin scolded. "You cannot do that. You have to come with me, your close relative, and remain with my mother until we meet your people."

The girl shook her head: "My mind is made up, so do not argue with me," she told him. "I am going to that camp of sacred nah-wak'-o-sis-grow-ers, and live with the finest girl I ever heard of, Dove Woman!"

"But you must n't! Just think what every one will say when they hear of your crossing the mountains alone with Black Elk!"

"I care not what they say! I know my personality. I have done nothing to shame me and never shall!" she cried.

"And I shall be as a real brother to her. Does any one doubt it?" cried I.

"A few last words to you, Crow Body, my

229

cousin," said she. "In this my time of trouble I could not bear the life of the great camp, its singing and dancing and feasting and laughter. Only in that little camp of earnest, praying growers of nah-wak'-o-sis do I feel that I can find the relief I seek, therefore to them I go."

"As you will, cousin, as you will," Crow Body replied. "And may you soon recover your peace of mind in that quiet camp. Do not forget that this past night we took nineteen scalps of the enemy, and that the body of the one who·wronged you is at the bottom of the river; that will be a healing thought."

"And now we part. May the gods preserve you both from all dangers," said Yellow Wolf, and called to the long column of riders and herders to move on.

We let them pass, followed them a little way, and then bore off to the left, leaving no traces of our departure from the big trail. Nor did we once travel in our trail during that day; we kept well out from it, and never stopped until night came. We picketed the horses in the best places that we could find for them, and, having no food, at once lay down and slept. We were very tired.

It was not until near sundown of the next day, when we were well up in the mountains, that I managed to kill some meat, a young whitetail buck; we surely needed it. I built a fire with my bow-drill and we roasted a quantity of the ribs and loins, and

I Enter the Dreadful Cave

I ate plenty, the girl sparingly; she was too heart-sick to enjoy food, and try as I would I could not succeed in my efforts to turn her thoughts to pleasant things.

We had no trouble of any kind in crossing the great range, and in the afternoon of our fourth day of hard traveling rounded the end of the big, red mountain of the Two Medicine, and the roar of the falls of the river cave broke upon our ears. I was so anxious to learn if all was well with my people that I would not stop to show my companion the dreadful place. We hurried on, passed the big beaver pond, and turned up the ridge, and sighted the little camp. There were my father and Old Sun, resting and smoking in the shade of a cottonwood; the women under another tree, busy with their different tasks, and the children playing about them. I was so glad to see them all that my eyes became misty. I raised the song of victory, and they sprang up and with outstretched arms came running to meet us. And then they saw that my companion was a woman, a young and beautiful woman, and they stopped short and stared at her, all the gladness vanishing instantly from their faces. But Antelope Woman paid no attention to their angry stares; she sprang from her horse and ran to Dove Woman, crying: "Oh, generous one! Pity me! Be good to me! Love me, poor one that I am!"

And Dove Woman? Why, she just reached out

and embraced the sobbing girl, and kissed her, and answered, as she smiled up at me: "Yes! Yes! Of course I shall love you! Whatever your troubles, they are ended now."

"Black Elk, what means this?" my mother demanded. "Have you deceived us — sneaked away to the North Blackfeet and taken a woman? And without so much as a word to your father and me of your intention! Oh, you without shame!"

"Not so," I laughed. "A Kalispel killed her man and stole her, and over there across the mountains One Horn and I killed him and rescued her from drowning. She is sick with grief. You must be good to her!"

"Oh, of course! Of course! Poor young widow!" she cried, and ran to the girl to comfort her. And at that my father and Old Sun and the women and children began to dance around me, calling out my name again and again and praising me for having counted *coup* upon the enemy.

As soon as I could make myself heard I inquired for Long Bear, and was told that he was down at the falls, watching for the Under-Water person. And food, yes, they had plenty of food; they had dried the bull meat and brought it home, and, a day back, Dove Woman had killed a fat bull elk close to camp. I looked off at our garden of nah-wak'-o-sis; the plants were almost as high as my knees; they would soon blossom. Truly, all was well with us.

I Enter the Dreadful Cave

We moved on to the shelter of the trees, and one of my almost-mothers led away the horses to picket them upon good grass; another hastened into our lodge to prepare food for me. Dove Woman had taken the young widow to her lodge, to comfort her as best she could. My father called upon me to relate all that I had seen and done over across the mountains. I did so, and they all rejoiced over the terrible blow that had been struck at the Kalispels.

Said Old Sun, when I had finished: "You can thank us, young warrior, that you have come safely through the dangers of that long trail. We made rich sacrifices for you; daily smoked and prayed the gods to keep you from all harm."

"I knew that you were doing that; it was a great comfort to me," I replied.

While relating my adventures I had all the time been aware of old Red Wing Woman's gleaming little eyes upon me, her lips set in a derisive grin, and well I knew that she was preparing to give me a shot with her too-ready tongue. It came: "Yes. The gods were more than good to you," she said. "They not only kept you safe from harm; they gave you a beautiful young companion for your homeward trail. What a gay time you must have had!"

I had not thought that she could say anything so mean as that. I could not make any reply to it; could only stare at her; and so it was with my father. But Old Sun was different; he was ever

233

The Dreadful River Cave

ready for a battle with words. He leaned forward and shook his fist at the old woman and roared: "You know that you have n't the slightest belief in what you hint! You are angry, jealous, because Dove Woman is giving a little of her loving heart to that poor girl-widow and so you try to make us all unhappy with you! Go away from us! Be ashamed of yourself!"

She arose and started off into the timber, crying mournfully. Dove Woman heard her, came out and ran to her side and petted her, and led her home. A little later she, too, was doing little kindnesses to the mourner.

"My son, women's ways are like the flight of the mud-house birds;[1] they dart hither and thither, never in any one direction; you can never predict whither they will go!" my father remarked.

"Yes?" my mother said, as she set food before me. "Well, when those mud-house birds are darting about so erratically in the air they are doing something: they are catching flies for their young!"

"Ha!" "H'm!" my father and Old Sun exclaimed. I laughed outright, and all the women laughed with me and scattered to their evening tasks.

Toward sundown I saw Long Bear returning and hurried out to meet him. We embraced; were very glad to be together again. We sat down and I told him as quickly as I could — and signs are much

[1] Swallows.

I Enter the Dreadful Cave

faster than words — all about my journey to the West. He was very much pleased with my success.

"I have big news for you," he signed to me when I had finished. "I have told no one about it, not even Dove Woman. Almost-brother, three days back, down at the falls, I saw that cave-dweller!"

"Good! Good! Quick, tell me all about it," I demanded.

"The sun had gone down; in the cañon it was almost dark. I was sitting behind the bushes watching — was about to sneak away from the place and start for home when I saw him. Out from the mist he came, down along the rocks on the far side of the falls, wrapped in a robe he was, and carried something under it. He came to a flat rock, laid aside his robe, and opened his bundle; it was his clothing and a bow-and-arrow case. He dressed, drew out his bow and strung it, took out several arrows, and slung the case upon his back, lifted his robe, and went up the cañon side and disappeared in the timber. Almost-brother, I could see him but dimly; it was quite dusk there in the cañon; but from what I did make out of his body, his actions, he seemed to me to be just a man of this earth. Are the Under-Water People like us, I wonder?"

"Why did you not tell my father and Old Sun about this?" I asked.

"The little camp was sad enough over your absence; I did not want to add to their worries," he answered.

The Dreadful River Cave

"Well, we will talk to them about it now," I said, and led the way to our lodge in which my mother was building a little evening fire. The old men had already come in, and I told them what Long Bear had seen, and asked if they still believed that the cave-dweller was an Under-Water person?

"We have no reason to believe that he is anything else," said Old Sun. "That ancient tale of ours, of our ancestor who visited the water-dwellers in their deep-down lodges, particularly states that, bodily, they are in no way different from us. But they have what we have not and can never have, the power to live in the water. And they surely hate us; never have we done them harm, yet they are always dragging us down to our death. Why, of course the cave-dweller is an Under-Water person; no man of the earth would live in that place of dreadful rushing, roaring water!"

"Old Sun, my friend, your words are my words: that sneaker in and out under the falls can be no other than an Under-Water person!"

"Well, be he what he may, if he is in that cave to-morrow he shall see my face!" I said.

Hearing that, my mother and all the women sat for a moment staring at me and then made great outcry, begging me to keep away from the falls and even from the cañon. My father frowned at them, motioned them to be quiet, and then said to me: "My son, we shall to-morrow make the most

I Enter the Dreadful Cave

powerful medicine for you that we can, and go
with you to the falls!"

"Ai! Ai! That which one has vowed to do, that
must he do!" Old Sun approved.

Behold me, then, early in the afternoon of that
never-to-be forgotten day, and fresh from a medicine sweat lodge, standing near the foot of the
falls and on the south side of the deep pool. Beside
me were my father and Old Sun, guns in hand.
Scattered along the opposite edge of the pool were
all the other members of our camp — even the
children — Dove Woman standing nearest the
falls and holding my gun, and Long Bear by her
side. I removed all my clothing, all but belt and
breechclout, stuck knife inside my belt, took up
my bow and four arrows — the sacred number —
and, with a last and silent appeal to the gods for
help, moved forward.

I had good footing upon the steep rocks at the
edge of the falls until I arrived at the first shelf in
the slant, and there saw that I should have to get
right into the water. Gripping my bow and arrows
firmly with my teeth, and grasping projections of
the rock wall with both hands, I stepped in, and
though the water was not halfway to my knees,
such was its force that it almost swept me off my
feet. I was here rounding a projection of the wall,
and before I passed was three times all but torn
from my holds upon it. Beyond that point the

The Dreadful River Cave

going was more easy—the water deeper, but less swift. On I went up the steep slant, passing quickly through the spray of the upper fall, so quickly that I knew my bowstring was not loosened, and then the light began to fail me. I arrived at the head of the falls and stepped from the water out upon a smooth and narrow shore of rock. Close ahead, at about the height of my waist, was the beginning of a flat shelf in the wall that I was following. The opposite wall, rising straight up from the water, was as smooth as ice, and so was the roof, close over my head.

I stood there a long time, trying to see into the far stretches of that dreadful place, and because I could not do so my courage began to fail me. I scolded myself. I said that I would have courage, and fitted an arrow to my bow and advanced along that narrow and slippery shore. And now, as I left behind me the roar of the falls, there came to my ears from the blackness ahead, frightful groanings and rumblings and hissings that I at first thought were the cries of the Under-Water People, preparing to attack me. Almost I turned back, then recognized them for what they were, the outcries of the river in its too close confinement. I moved on to the shelf, took bow and arrows in my right hand and felt across it with my left — not quite the length of my arm — and found that it, too, was ice-smooth.

From there I went on more and more slowly and

238

I Enter the Dreadful Cave

into deeper and deeper darkness, feeling my way along the narrow shore with my feet, and with my left hand hard-pressing the shelf for support in case I should step off into deep water. I could look back and see every part of the way that I had come from the head of the falls, but looking ahead, my eyes were of no more use than those of a blind man. I could not even see my hand as I slid it along the shelf. Nor could I see the river, flowing swiftly at my side.

In this manner I had gone on for some distance, perhaps thirty or forty steps, when my hand slid against something that I instantly knew did not belong upon that shelf; something soft and crinkly-haired — a buffalo robe! Ha! How my heart jumped! I drew back my hand to seize the bow and arrows which all the time I had been holding in my right hand, and as I did so, I heard a faint rustling close ahead, as of some one sliding down off the shelf. I fitted an arrow to the bow and raised it, and it was knocked out of my hand and I received a stinging knife stab in the upper part of my left arm, a stab that would likely have pierced my breast had it not been deflected by the bow. I lunged forward and grappled with my enemy and pressed his knife arm close against his side. But with his free hand he seized me by the throat and began choking me. His warm breath was in my face; my bare body was pressing against him, a man of no great size, who had on shirt and

The Dreadful River Cave

leggings and moccasins of leather that was dry.
Dry!

"Ha! This is no Under-Water person, he is a
real person!" I said to myself, and great courage
came to me. I felt strong. I struggled hard to get
possession of his knife — I could not draw mine —
and stab him before he could shut off my wind.
And suddenly we slipped from that narrow shore
into the swift-running river!

As we struck the water the man let go of my
throat and tried to free himself from my embrace.
Even if we parted I knew that I could not escape
the falls, and determined to hold him so that his
body should shield mine from the upstanding rocks
in that fearful plunge. I found bottom with my
feet and gave a spring and a whirl and brought him
around in front of me, and had no more than done
that than we were at the mouth of the cave and
going over the edge of the falls.

Somewhere on the way down that roaring, foaming, slanting plunge my living shield struck a rock
with such force that he was almost torn from my
arms. As we whirled from the rock I became the
shield for him; but we were then going down into
the depths of the pool, and more and more slowly
as we neared the bottom. Down there the water
seemed to be drawing us all ways at once and with
resistless force. My back rubbed along some slippery stones, and then a swirling, heaving current
pushed us swiftly toward the surface. I felt air

WE WERE AT THE MOUTH OF THE CAVE AND GOING OVER
THE EDGE OF THE FALLS

I Enter the Dreadful Cave

upon my face and opened my eyes as I took a deep breath, and found myself staring up at Dove Woman, holding my gun out to me. I seized it with one hand, and grasped the hair of my limp enemy with the other; she drew me to shore and then with Long Bear's help dragged my enemy out of the water. There was a deep wound in the back of his head; his wide-open eyes were motionless; he was dead! Oh, how the women and children yelled as they came crowding around us, and, across, my father and Old Sun raised the victory song as they hurried down the shore to the fording-place and splashed through the water and came up and stared at the body.

"Why, he is no Under-Water person!" my father cried. "Look at his clothing, the white men's knife in his hand. And the quill embroidery on his moc-casins — why, I know that pattern! He is a Snake man!"

"That he is!" Old Sun roared. "A Snake! Now I am angry! I thought that, at last, I was actually to see an Under-Water person! I shall never see one! Oh, how angry-disappointed I am!"

But none of us felt that way; we were very happy.

It was with the greatest difficulty that I took the knife from my dead enemy's stiffened hand, and then I thought of my bow, and cried out that I had lost it. Lo! One of my little brothers had seen it drifting down along the shore and had rescued it.

The Dreadful River Cave

My father had brought over my clothes. I put them on.

We could not keep our eyes off the dead man. Said my mother: "Well, he was an enemy, but I can't help it: I pity him. And I wonder why he was living in that dreadful river cave."

"For that he — his shadow — should have praise," said my father. "He was undoubtedly there to obtain a vision from his gods, and none but a very brave man would have dared enter the black hole."

"Ai! And his gods must have been gods of the water. Well, we will give him to them," said Old Sun, and slid the body back into the pool. And with that we turned and took the trail for home.

Well, my son, I have but little more to say. After my encounter with the vision-seeker, our days were quiet and happy enough there in the valley of the Two Medicine. If enemies entered it, we never saw them. Our sacred plants grew fast. Long Bear's arm mended and grew strong, and he hunted with me. At the appointed time our people came for us and we harvested our large crop of nah-wak'-o-sis with great ceremony and prayers and rejoicings. The young widow, somewhat recovered from her grief, left us to live with her aunt until we should meet the North Blackfeet. And then, one evening, I gave Long Bear the horses that I had promised him, and said that we should miss

I Enter the Dreadful Cave

him very much when he returned to his people. He made no reply to that; just looked across the lodge and smiled at Dove Woman. And she said, so low that we could no more than hear her:

"He is not going back to his people; we are to set up a lodge of our own."

"Oh, my children!" old Red Wing Woman cried. "You have the lodge now; my lodge. I give it to you! Oh, how glad-feeling I am that I am to have a grandson so kind, so brave!"

"Ha! Now I am surprised!" Old Sun exclaimed. "Red Wing Woman, for the first time in my life, I hear you approving something. It must be that you are not well!"

And then were we all surprised, for she answered him not one word.

After me, so far as I know, but one other person ever entered the dreadful river cave, and that person was a girl. No other than she who became our virgin woman warrior, she to whom we gave a man-name, Running Eagle. Lying there upon the rock shelf in the dark cave she fasted and prayed and got a powerful vision, powerful medicine, and became a brave and successful leader of some of our war parties. That is why we name the place Running Eagle Falls and Running Eagle Cave.

Oh, my son! Would that I could live again that summer in the Two Medicine Valley! But, in a way, I have lived it again in telling you about it. You

The Dreadful River Cave

have written it all down, and your white people will read the story. That is good; it is right that they should know something of the full and happy life we led in the long ago — in the time before they overran our country and killed off our game!

THE END

The Riverside Press

CAMBRIDGE . MASSACHUSETTS

U . S . A